AFRICAN WISDOM

AFRICAN WISDOM

Ifeanyi Uhuegbu

LitPrime Solutions
21250 Hawthorne Blvd
Suite 500, Torrance, CA 90503
www.litprime.com
Phone: 1-800-981-9893

Published by LitPrime Solutions: 07/26/2023

ISBN: 979-8-88703-126-2(sc)
ISBN: 979-8-88703-127-9(e)

Library of Congress Control Number: 2022923913

Contents

PART 2

PART 3

Dedication

I WOULD LIKE TO EXPRESS MY sincere thanks to my wonderful wife Dikachim who gave me all the support and the encouragement to write this book.

I wish to specifically thank Reverend Dr. Richard Udoh and wife Rita for identifying the potentials. They pressed it on me that I have something on the inside which the world would like to read and the result is this book.

PART 1

Chapter One

INTRODUCTION

Stories are part of the African life. Africans relish narratives and telling stories. These are often deployed to teach lessons and pass messages of values. Proverbs are fundamental to the stories. They are vehicles used most times to drive home the importance of the stories.

Scenes of people gathered in the villages under the moonlight telling stories are common in Africa. They are a way of life. The ability to tell stories coherently and articulately is highly respected in the traditional African society. Most often, the intelligent quotient of a child can be identified and developed through this means.

Ability to use proverbs and appropriately in moonlight gatherings, folklores, dances, and conversations as well as in songs in various village activities is well regarded. No wonder, at many of these occasions the elders participate in telling the stories, thereby educating the young ones both in the art of storytelling and in history. This setting that combines a deep acculturation process is captured in the saying that when the mother goat is chewing cud, the kids watch the mouth. The young ones learn the art of storytelling and use of proverbs in this way. It is part of the socialization process.

Proverbs are indeed second nature to the elders in the African society. They use them freely during conversations and in story telling. The recognition of this situation is reflected in the culture in which any one person who applies proverbs in the course of speaking in the presence of the elders often adds "as our elders said" or "as you elders would say it".

The idea in this, is to give reverence to the elders present and also acknowledge the source of the proverb being used. It would be rude for a young person to pretend to be teaching the elders the use of proverbs. Such acknowledgements help the child when he uses a harsh or vulgar proverb. It saves the young person from incurring the wrath of the elders.

Proverbs are the lubricant of any good conversation. At public meetings, crucial consultations, marriages, funerals, sundry social events and in such formal correspondences as sending emissaries to a foreign land, proverbs are profusely used. The ability to use proverbs adequately and freely in many African societies is a big credential for recognition and for entrusting people with responsibility of speaking for group or community. The capacity to wrap messages in proverbs is a reflection of maturity and wisdom or tendencies in those directions.

*When the mother goat is chewing
cud, the little ones watch her.*

Proverbs mainly derive their substance from the culture of the people. Just as African cultures are rich, colourful and diverse, so also are their proverbs. But a close look at each culture's body of proverbs often reveals common link with others. For sure there are common grounds, even in experiences. The experiences which evolve from the distinct heritage of each culture form the foundation from which proverbs flow.

Usage of proverbs covers every aspect of life and living. There is virtually no issue or circumstance in the African world that does not have an appropriate proverb around it. Such proverbs may have evolved after careful observations spanning a long time. African proverbs are profound words of wisdom which reveal African philosophies.

In the setting in which they prevail, proverbs are believed to be said to the wise. However, for the sake of the less than wise and the young minds, ordinary prose becomes handy. This is the root of the saying that "If it were not for fools, conversations would have been only in proverbs". The point here is that the wise does not need too many words to grasp a message. An appropriate proverb is enough for any wise mind to receive the message being communicated. A good proverb stimulates thought, gives understanding, knowledge and entertains.

Usually it is considered superfluous, if not an outright blunder when a man who communicated proverbially, is also made to break them down. To expect that of any speaker is to ask for too much. On the other hand, it doesn't speak well of any recipients of proverbs communication to ask the communicator to decode it. Such conduct exposes a message receiver as being less than wise. Consequently, it is said that "When a man who spoke in proverbs goes ahead to interpret them to the recipient, the dowry paid on the recipient mother's during marriage was a waste." A testimonial for a person does not get worse than that. It is an indication that the person did not receive proper home training. Such an unwise person is often a subject of ridicule.

....

**_If it were not for fools conversations
would be in proverbs._**

....

Proverbs are believed to be no respecter of persons. They could be sublime and come in various forms. Some could ordinarily be considered interrogative while some are rhetorical. Yet some come in rather plain vulgar form. Intended message and circumstances dictate the appropriateness of a proverb. The most important thing in a proverb usage is that the intended message is clear enough not to leave the receiver conjecturing the actual meaning.

Proverbs are as dynamic as culture. They could be fashioned to suit changes in the society. Contemporary developments in African cultures have given rise to many proverbs. It is said in a more modern phrase for instance that: "A man who does not have money to buy stout beer often deride the drink as being too bitter."

Stout beer is of course, a relatively new beverage in the African society. Prior to the arrival of the European, otherwise referred to as White man in Africa, stout beer was not part of the stock of drink in the society. Alcoholic beverages as they originally came in the setting were mainly palm wine and such local brews as pinto, *brukutu. Akpetesi* amongst others.

What is important in the proverb in reference is the message; that most people without the means to acquire a particular commodity or item are usually dismissive of that which they cannot afford. It often comes easily to people to wave off what they do not have.

As with culture which is hardly outgrown by its own, nobody outgrows proverbs. They are always there for application when relevant. In fact, the older one gets the closer the hug with proverbs. That way they are passed down from generation to generation through oral tradition.

It is hardly the case that any parent sits his child down to teach him the art of using or speaking in proverbs. No parent sends the child to school to learn proverbs.

The acculturation in proverb deployment comes mainly through experiencing its usage, usually by the older and wiser people. Reading books on proverbs as a guide to their use is a latter-day source of acquiring knowledge about proverbs. This means is however, still not a common route to learning use of this deft communication skill.

There are no fast rules to the application of proverbs in a conversation or writing. They can be employed at the beginning, middle or end of any conversation. Whether a proverb comes in form of a story or question is determined by context or thrust of the message. It is all at the discretion of the user. The important thing is to have them effectively propel the transmission of a desired message to the audience.

A proverb wrongly used can cause more problem than the good it was meant to achieve. That is the basis of the saying that "A slip of the tongue is more dangerous than a slip of the foot." That is to say, an unruly tongue can cause an irreparable damage to a good cause.

Here the eternal advice of the bible comes in useful; that it is better to be quick to listen, slow to speak and slow to get angry. The bible also notes that although the tongue is a small member of the body, it can cause a lot of havoc. "A tiny spark," the holy book says "can set a great forest on fire".

It is better to either remain quiet or use plain language in a conversation or presentation than for someone to use a proverb that doesn't fit. Such faux pas may be unpardonable. Therefore, it is counseled that anyone who is not adept at the application of proverbs should do well to be smart as the proverbial man who on being called up to speak at a public forum said his kinsmen have said it all. Such is deemed more honourable than to speak and exhibit lack of proper grounding.

It remains common today in the African societies to find orators; politicians, preachers, various categories of salesmen, and many others using proverbs extensively to pass their messages to their respective publics. This disposition is not for nothing. Proverbs leave catchy phrases and messages that sink with the individual or the targeted audience and subsequently may make them draw a reflection and respond to the information communicated. They act as the engine oil in conversations, making their users apply them freely while scoring points along the line. Proverbs are catalysts for conversations, dialogue, and public discourse.

A slip of the tongue is more dangerous than a slip of the foot.

The adage that "if a child washes his hands well, he dines with the elders" manifests clearly in the use of proverbs in Africa. A child who has learned the apt usage of proverbs is revered and elevated above his peers in the society. In many gatherings, such a young person is often easily granted audience whenever he wants to speak. He may sometimes be given responsibilities at the expense of his seniors and those more educated in western style.

Good usage of proverbs depicts wisdom. And wisdom, according to the bible, is the foundation of life. In fact, it is life. King Solomon was regarded as the wisest man of his era. That reckoning as the wisest of men still subsists. He was famed for churning out about 3,000 proverbs. These are still as profound and relevant today as they were thousands of years back. Such is the eternal depth of proverbs.

Without doubt, the proverbs of Solomon which were inspired by God have stood the test of time and are still standing in time. While it is a fact that proverbs are living and dynamic, it is a fact that many witty proverbs of the modern times have proved far less enduring than old ones. Indeed, many modern proverbs have been vacated by circumstances that have proven them wrong. Many of them are coined out of human experiences and insight and are bound to disappoint sometimes.

Messages and sense in most proverbs are weighty when set in the context of time and society in which they were fashioned out. Preferably, proverbs are best used in the original language in which they were framed. Many proverbs lose their actual meaning in the course of effort to translate them to either English or any other foreign language. There are native words and idioms that cannot be easily substituted with English words.

The determination to avoid distortion that may

follow such translation from an original language to a second one accounts for the retention of Latin words and phrases in various official documents and communications. The idea is to retain the exact meaning of a particular expression as was intended in the original language of the construction.

Chapter Two

PROVERBS: BUSINESS OF THE ELDERS

When I told a friend and colleague from Kenya, Pastor John Nganga that I was writing a book on 'African proverbs', the first question he asked was "How old are you? Pastor Nganga's reaction was not exactly new to me. Amongst my peers and relations, each time I use a proverb in conversation, the common reaction is always the raising of eye brows. The next thing that follows is the question: Why are you always talking like an old man? Many of those who know me well enough and are convinced that I am not the old man as my proverbs reflect simply hold that I must have been brought up under the tutelage of an old man.

Truly I grew up under several elderly relations, men, and women. As a little boy growing up, I loved listening to moonlight stories and talks delivered by the elders in village gatherings and meetings. My interest was nourished the more through reading novels and plays by African writers, especially Chinua Achebe, Cyprian Ekwensi, and Ola Rotimi among others. Studying Theatre Arts and Journalism in my first and post graduate studies in the university gave me another opportunity to develop much desires for the use of proverbs.

Are proverbs really the exclusive right of the elders? While the answer may not be an emphatic yes, it remains a fact that the elders are more adept in deploying them and indeed make use of proverbs more than any other demographic segment in any African society. They use them profusely in discussions, meetings, counseling, admonishing, in diplomacy and all phases of life. They are not only custodians of cultures; they are also proverb custodians. It does not mean there are no young men proficient in the use of proverbs. However, the truth is that any young person skilled in the use of proverbs must have learned it through good associations with the elders.

It is easy to appreciate therefore, why most times young people presage their use of proverbs in the presence of an elder with "it is you elders who said..." Or "our elders said". This is a tribute to the wisdom of the elders as well as an acknowledgement that they are the repository of tradition and wisdom.

Though it is said that "a widely traveled child is more knowledgeable than a grey haired elder in the village," that does not translate into approval for a child to disrespect his elders. The elders deserve their respect. It is part of the African cultural heritage.

It is generally believed in Africa that respect for the elders is ultimately in the interest of the young ones. For as the saying holds, "when a child accords respect to elders, he will grow up to become one." This is in tandem with the fifth of the Ten Commandments of the Christian faith which says "honour your father and mother. Then you will live a long full life in the land the Lord your God will give." This is the only commandment with a promise. Our "father and mother" in the broad sense usage here is easily accepted to refer to any elders or equivalent of our biological parents.

A widely traveled child is more knowledgeable than a grey haired elder in the village.

Elders are commonly believed to have wisdom and experience. The is naturally derived from several years of practical life lessons as well as being witness to varied circumstances of life. Experience is often difficult to quantify and cannot be abridged. It remains the best teacher. The value of experience is highlighted regularly in media advertisements for job employment opportunities. The emphasis in such advertisements to the effect that a certain number of years' experience is an advantage for securing the job says it all for the inherent value in experience. Experience is an important part of human existence. By virtue of age, the elders have experiences of life in their kitty. This advantage enhances their position as custodians of culture and traditions in every African society.

Expectedly, many proverbs have been woven around the elders. The proverbs convey a lot of wisdom and instructions for all to learn. After all, it is said that the words of elders are words of wisdom. A wise man hears them and becomes wiser.

The elevated status of the African elders in terms of taking responsibility manifests clearly in the saying that "an elder cannot be at home while a goat tethered to a stake delivers." Any such occurrence reflects the worst type of abdication of responsibility and bothers on an abomination. In other words, elders are expected to correct any wrong conduct right away or indeed prevent them from occurring in the first place. Such is the responsibility society entrusts on their shoulders.

An elder who decides to keep quiet in the face of wrong doings often loses the respect of the society. The seriousness with which society views expectations of corrective conduct from elders is reflected in the saying that "if an elder is witness to an evil and refuses to speak up, when death comes it will claim the elder first. But if he speaks out and the young ones refuse to listen to him, death will claim them first before the elder."

Though he is expected to speak with wisdom, an

elder at the same time is not expected to speak always. There is wisdom in speaking few words and in listening. Silence is golden, after all, at least sometimes. In the art of communication especially in the traditional African setting, it often pays to listen more and speak little.

It is also said that "an elder does not speak with all the sides of his mouth." An elder who is loquacious and full of words discovers sooner or later that his words have gradually lost weight and value. Such an elder is seen eventually as a talkative. It is true of course, that the more words one speaks, the more vulnerable he is bound to be, through slips and various mistakes. There is wisdom in keeping quiet sometimes while others do the talking.

Unfortunately, there are instances where some elders have debased their status because of material consideration. Even within the very communal setting of traditional African society, some elders are known to pervert justice after accepting inducements or gratification.

The prospect faced by any such erring elder walking the path of untruth and injustice is captured in the saying that "if an elder makes himself a common commodity, even children will pick him up" Succinctly put, if an elder abuses his right, he gets abuses from even the smallest child in the community. Another proverb that captures the same message holds that "an elder who lowers himself has given a licence to little children to ride him".

Furthermore, it is said in connection to the society's

expectations from the elders that "When highly respected elders can jettison honour for the devil's money, of course dogs will eat shame and men will eat faeces. "This is a twist depicting a world turned upside down. There are different laws governing men and animals. If man starts being governed by the law of animals which brings out the bestiality in him because of ephemeral material needs, reactions that are uncommon invariably follow. That is the message.

Over time, as the African society steadily loses its traditional values, elders have been dropping from their hitherto Olympian height. Indeed, many elders today have thrown caution to the wind. They have compromised their highly exalted position on the altar of greed, avarice, and poverty. The decline in the values and culture in contemporary African societies can be understood from this angle. "Indeed dog has eaten the bone hung on the neck".

An elder who lowers himself gives license to little children to ride him.

Across the present African societies of this age, in Nigeria for example, many elders have jettisoned the restraint and dignity of their station in life and are now found in strange positions. They not only give judgments that are tainted, some are commonly found fraternizing with younger elements whose sources of wealth are highly questionable. Among the loud *nouveau riche* that litters the Nigerian society for instance, there are ample instances of some who cannot even write their names and whose wealth has no known sources, but who have found themselves being bestowed with high traditional titles. The magic wand is money and some elders endorse the rut. In certain instances, such abuse of the values of the society occurs when it was apparent that the elements concerned were identified with antisocial and criminal cases as serious as armed robbery, kidnapping, ritual murders, and assassinations. Such is the degeneration and denigration of our values and cultures today encouraged by some elders. But these aberrations have not wiped away the wisdom and respect of old age.

Chapter Three

THE CONCEPT OF GOD

"WHEN A MAN SAYS YES, his god also says yes." That is a popular maxim in the lgbo culture in Africa. It is an affirmation of faith in God. It may not have been faith in the almighty as we know Him today. In many traditional African societies, the perception of God was of a being too mighty for ordinary mortals to approach Him directly. So, God was approached through various mediums and intermediaries. The procedure recognized the existence of a supreme deity who controls the affairs of men and must be believed before any petition can be entertained by him.

This belief with few modifications finds commonality with the modern Christian concept of fellowship with God. Our relationship with God is only made possible through faith. The bible says that anyone that comes to God must first of all believe that he exists and he rewards those that seek him diligently.

Equally, the bible says (Hebrews 1I v 6) *"Without faith it is impossible to please God..."*

Life in itself is a challenge. Man's ability to sustain faith that he is capable of surmounting odds goes a long way in making him victorious. Life is all about faith. There is nothing we receive from God that is not based on faith. That is the substance of our relationship with him. Sometimes we exercise faith without knowing it. Our faith is more emphasized when we are confronted with bigger challenges in life.

However, there are people who still believe that they can run the race of life all alone. Whatever success such people have achieved so far, they attribute to their ingenuity, doggedness and wisdom. The saying that "whoever begins a race without putting God in the front will run forever" makes the ultimate likelihood of such people achieving full success doubtful.

Indeed, there is nothing that is made in this world without God knowing. Embarking on any venture without God is akin to embarking on a journey to a foreign land without a road map. The adventurer is bound to wander for life without reaching his destination. Many who embarked on many ventures and arrogated their success to themselves soon discovered in the words of King Solomon that life can end up as vanity upon vanity and vexation of the spirit. It is God that gives satisfaction in life. He is the giver of bread to the eater, and seed to the sower.

Winning the battles of this life is not by power, nor by might. Not on the basis of our intelligence. It is by the grace of God. There are so many strong and intelligent people who never succeeded in their calling. Yet there are many people nobody gave an iota of chance to succeed but they became victorious.

***

***Whoever begins a race
without putting God in the
front will run forever.***

***

Perhaps this informed the wise words in Ecclesiastes 9 v. 11 that the fastest runner doesn't always win the race, and the strongest warrior doesn't always win the battle. The wise are often poor and the skillful are not necessarily wealthy. Being well educated does not always lead to a successful life. It is all decided by fate, by being at the right place at the right time. "These are factors controlled by God. It is therefore foolhardy for anyone to boast of achieving anything out of his own effort.

A relevant adage here holds that "When the lizard abandons the iroko tree, it becomes easy for the predators to apprehend it". This is a warning to those who feel they can run the race of life on their own without God. They will simply be exposing themselves to the enemy who sooner than later takes them captive.

The belief in God's overwhelming control of human

activities is strong in Africa. Atheism and the various philosophical inclinations common in the Western hemisphere have virtually no ground in African societies. The Akans in Ghana, (West Africa) expressed the disapproval for atheism aptly in the proverb: "No one shows God to a child." Just as the Patriarch Abraham in the bible account paid tithe and homage to Melchizedek, the King of Salem, in recognition of the great and wonderful things he has done, the existence of God is too obvious for any of us to see. Even the blind can 'see' and feel the existence of God. The saying touches the profundity of God in the life of all creations as personified by children who do not yet have analytical mind of their own.

Another proverb points out that "If you run away from God, you are still under him". This simply underlines the omnipresence and omnipotence of God. Anyone doubting the existence of God is merely engaged in foolish trip, for such a person surely enjoys God's moonlight, sunlight, rainfall, vegetations, air and all the good things he has decorated this world with.

The proverb is also a warning that there is no hiding place for the sinner. The bible alerts in Proverb 15 v 3 that "The Lord is watching everywhere, keeping his eye on both the evil and the good."

Africans strongly believe in the intervention of God in the affairs of man. When man's efforts have failed him there is always the unseen hand which intervenes. In Greek mythology, it is known as Deus ex machina. Thus, it is often said in Africa that: "God is never asleep." He is awake always to fight for his children, setting the captives free. He stays in his heavenly abode and watches us daily; our goings and comings, our pains and joys. God intervenes when man's hopes have failed him. He does the miraculous.

The saying is true that "no man can out give God". Even when we do not recognize him, he still blesses us. While we were yet sinners, he gave us his son Jesus Christ to die at the cross of Calvary. And through that singular act, we now have life and more abundantly too. No matter what we give to God, we cannot match his generosity towards us.

Giving is a spiritual process. The bible says it is better to give than to receive. In simple practical life expressions, the hand that gives is always on top. Many locked doors are unlocked when we give cheerfully and generously to those from whom we are not expecting anything in return.

It is now common to find many Pentecostal pastors exploiting the concept of giving to extort money from members of their congregations. They back their greed with quotes from the scriptures that exhorts one to *give and it shall be given unto you good measure, pressed drown, shaken together and running over. So shall men give unto our bossom.*

While this is important, salvation and righteousness which should form the pillar of Christianity are often not emphasized by this school of preachers. This inclination is wrong. The truth is that when a man's soul is converted, it is easy to convert the pocket and bank account. However, the truth is that no matter what we give to God we are just returning part of the bountiful blessings he has decorated us with. Therefore let no one be weary in giving.

For those who arrogate so much power to themselves, it is important to come to terms with the proverb: "No matter how strong a great man is, he should never challenge his personal god". Our personal god is our guardian angel. He knows everything about us; our strength and weakness. It would amount to a great disaster if anyone decides to challenge what sustains him. This will tantamount to playing God. God cannot of course, share his glory with anyone. Herod tried it in the bible and he was eaten up by worms.

> **No matter how strong a great man is, he should never challenge his personal god.**

The builders of the great ship, Titanic had reportedly boasted that "God himself could not sink this ship". The ship, with a name derived from the great Greek god, was designed to live up to its splendour and awe. It was the biggest passenger ship ever built then. But the gigantic Titanic was man made. It sank into the icy waters of the North Atlantic Ocean in 1912. The fate of the ship buttressed the fact that God is almighty and cannot be challenged.

Chapter Four

PROVERBS AS MIRROR OF THE SOCIETY

THE AIM OF EVERY COMMUNICATION is to deliver home a message and possibly achieve some understanding. Proverbs bring about understanding if well applied. A well used proverb can stimulate thoughts, bring about understanding, facilitates counseling, diplomacy and conflict resolutions. Proverbs often reflect the mores, values, beliefs and social fabric of the society.

The values of the African societies which revere old age for instance is amply reflected in proverbs. The pre-eminent position of elders is such that No matter the gravity of their offence or shortcoming, it is still often the case that publicly confronting them is not deemed right. It is rather advised that appeal be made to an elder, directly or through a medium. You can now imagine what will become of a young man who decides to confront an elder to the extent of physically lifting him up. The proverb is therefore definite that "when a child lifts his father up, the father's wrapper blindfolds him." The blindfolding here is figurative. The reference is a warning that any such grossly disrespectful child can hardly move forward with such moral burden.

Africans believe that children are not the concern of only their very parents. Children belong to the community. So, whoever sees a child going astray has the right to call him to order by disciplining him in love. If a misbehaving child is not called to order and he grows up with anti-social behaviour, the family, community and the larger society will suffer the consequences. This orientation informed the saying that "when you see a fowl scattering droppings chase it away for nobody knows who will eat the legs when the fowl is turned to meat." Aligned to the above saying is another that says: "when an evil practice stays long, it becomes a culture". The proverb is a call to nip any anti-social behaviour in the bud before it becomes a monster which can consume everybody.

Put in another way "if you notice a growing stalk that can pierce the eye, you uproot it you don't sharpen it". This is a clarion call for all to join forces in removing every bad trait that is potentially dangerous to all. We should not ignore any evil practice going on around us. It is no good either to ignore an unwholesome practice because someone else is likely to be the victim. Sooner or later, the damage spreads.

It is believed in Africa that individualism and pampering of children are good, but only to an extent.

....

When an evil practice stays long, it becomes a culture.

....

The tendency to condone all conducts of children, including obnoxious ones is commonly perceived in the African societies as a major problem that threatens to destroy the moral fabric of Western cultures. A setting where children cannot be cautioned or smacked for going astray; where people live by the rule of law and not culture and where the law has been over amplified above culture eventually lead to consequences of increase in anti-social and criminal acts.

Perhaps one reason why it is good to nip any bad behaviour in the bud is because "when one finger touches oil it soils others". A bad behaviour spreads quickly like a wild fire in the harmattan. And when such bad behaviour prevails for a long time, people are bound to see it as a norm of the society.

African societies recognize hard work as a veritable way of promoting people into higher responsibilities. In this social environment, achievements are based on verifiable hard work. Currently there is an increase in celebrating those whose means of wealth are highly questionable. This group of people are being promoted into positions of higher responsibility. This is an error.

But families that still fear God and are worth their salt still insist that their young ones should be properly brought up and those who honestly achieved wealth and fame should be rewarded. Such families insist that their young ones must follow the right path of honour. There are no short cuts or arriving through the back door if the goal of honesty must be achieved. The danger in an impressionable mind turning a wrong bend is captured in the saying that "when a goat that does not eat yam starts keeping the company of the one that eats yam, it soon starts eating it." The idea here is that bad communication and influence corrupt good manners.

Of course, individual favours and destiny are not the same. Therefore, when one child follows another in perpetrating evil, the follower may fall into deeper mess whereas the one that initiated the wrong may get reprieve. It is often asked rhetorically therefore that "if the rat follows the lizard to run in the rain, when the body of the lizard dries up will that of the rat also dry?" Of course, the body texture of the rat is such that when it gets drenched, it can not dry immediately because of its hairs. That is different from the lizard with its scaly body. Such is the difference in outcome when we join others in doing evil. The initiator of the wrong act may go free while the convert shares a different fortune.

Where a young person or even an adult rejects or resists taking correction, the person may be reminded of the proverb that it is not only a dead person's neck that needs straightening, that of the living does need it too. Nobody is above correction. We are all mortals and fallible.

Another caution that has remained ever relevant is for each person to be circumspect in what he says and how he says it. The ability of each person to guard his mouth is very important as most strives in human societies have their root in idle words. The description of the tongue as a very small but dangerous member of the body is therefore very apt. The tongue carries the power of life and death. Often those who utter words with grave implications do not appreciate the gravity of what they do. It is said therefore that "when a little boy hides under the cover of the night to speak atrocities and abominations, he thinks there will be no dawn". The day must break to fulfil its command from God Almighty.

For quarrelling relations, the proverb that "the teeth and tongue are too close to litigate between themselves", is a weighty warning and a reminder. Good and mild words pacify anger and stop quarrels.

Proper applications of proverbs or oratorical skills help in resolving disputes. If we weigh our words before speaking them, if we appreciate that there is power in the tongue, then we will be much more mindful of every word we speak. And the society will be very much better for it.

....

**_The teeth and tongue are too close
to litigate between themselves._**

....

Chapter Five

MARRIAGE PROVERBS

MARRIAGE IS SEEN IN AFRICA as one of the means through which an individual is certified responsible member of the society. Africans celebrate marriage ceremonies with funfair, a disposition which underlies the importance attached to it. The community as one is usually involved in both the ceremony of marriage and the bond ensured by the relationship.

The great importance attached to the marriage institution and the ceremonies that go with it are the basis of many proverbs. Many of these are designed to promote and preserve the institution. For those inclined to pre-marital sex for instance, the saying is there that "Marriage is not palm wine to be tasted." This tendency is frowned at in the traditional African society.

In Africa, especially in the tropical rainforest belt, raffia and palm trees are tapped to produce a popular fermented drink called palm wine. It is rich in yeast and forms a major ingredient in marriage ceremonies. Palm wine intoxicates when consumed in excess. By its nature, the more days the drink is allowed to stay and ferment, the more intoxicating it becomes.

> **Marriage is not palm
> wine to be tasted.**

The usual practice before buying palm wine is to taste it. The idea is to find out how fresh the drink is, or whether it has soured over time. This pre-purchase sampling is not only allowed by the custom, it is a part of it. Unlike the palm wine, however, marriage is not made for pre-contractual testing. The virtue of virginity and sanctity in the young people going into marriage is highly extolled.

Apart from the shame that is associated with wanton loss of virginity, which could lead to a young lady being ridiculed and looked down on with some disdain, pre-marital loss of virginity could in some extreme social settings lead to death in some communities that emphasize virginity test. Such virginity test varies. In some communities, the ceremonies are performed with a life cock. The cock is handed over to the bride. If it dies in her hand, the evidence was conclusive that she was not a virgin.

In another vein, immediately after the marriage ceremony, the couple is locked up in a room where a bed has been made already with a white bed sheet. The groom is expected to present the white bed sheet with some blood stain after meeting his Wife as a sign that she was a virgin and he, the husband was the winner of the trophy.

Where the bride was a virgin, it enhanced her status in the community as a well brought up lady. The parents of such a virtuous lady will be highly respected and regarded for properly bringing up their daughter. Virginity of a bride in the traditional African society matters much and it engenders good social relationship between her family and the in-laws. Such warm relationship often provided the basis for expansion of the ties in various ways. As the saying goes "when a road appears nice, it encourages people to thread it more often." This could mean that a lady who preserved her virginity for her husband enables her husband to love her more. Similarly, the saying could mean that many people would like to marry from the family or community that produced such virtuous lady. Such a lady is not just a pride to her parents, she is an ambassador to her community.

When a lady's father or relative is opposed to her getting married, this proverb may be applied "no matter how beautiful a lady may be, the father cannot marry her." It is a taboo, an abomination for any father to marry the daughter. Even close relations up to the fourth generation are not allowed to marry.

The proverb also advises that there are certain things we cannot do by virtue of the position we occupy. It may be seen as patronizing or nepotism.

For those who go into marriage because of the beauty of the bride or the material things the groom expects to gain, the elders have some words of wisdom. It is cautioned that "the beauty of a woman is her character." And character is not visible at first sight. True beauty and character manifests in time, testified by behaviour and conduct.

No matter how beautiful a woman may appear if she lacks good manners, she is like a white sepulcher.

What makes up any human being is not found on the outside alone but mainly from within. Appearance is not real. The being, our inner part is what we use in relating with God and it is the most important aspect of our lives.

"Those who do not have forgiving spirit should not bother about marriage", is a saying used to encourage spouses in Africa to be tolerant of one another. Marriage is for forgivers. It is a union of two imperfect people who are aspiring for perfection. None of them is above board. As the couple drive through the highway of imperfection into "perfection" mistakes are made, corrections are carried out and lessons are learned. Anyone who does not know how to forgive should not venture into marriage.

Late Bishop Benson Idahosa, founder of Church of God Mission Incorporated once said; "Marriage is an institution no one graduates from". The bishop who popularized prosperity ministry in Africa was pointing out the fact that couples learn every day in a marriage. None of them should assume that the other knows it all. It is the daily surprises that make marriage interesting and sustaining.

For a marriage to last, it is said that "A mother in-law should be blind and deaf." Many marriages have been ruined by mother in-laws. A lot of them choose wife for their son. They tell their son how he should marry the wife. Thus, negating the biblical injunction that a man will leave the parents and cleave to the wife and the two shall become one body. Except a mother in-law decides to pretend to be blind and deaf by over looking some of the happenings in the son's marriage and equally not paying attention to all that is said, that marriage will crash.

*Marriage is an institution
no one graduates from.*

Of course, many marriages have crashed because of this problem. Some men are too attached to their mother's apron strings that it looks as if their mother is competing with their wives for a dose of their love. Due to the prevailing condition where many young men in marriage acting like boys and are controlled by their mothers, some young ladies detest getting married to such "baby-men" whose mothers are still alive. They prefer orphans, at least no one will brainwash their husbands. It is jovially said that ladies in this group often put on a sort of scarf that comes low close to their eyes. It is a symbolic statement and tagged "not interested in having mother in-law." What a shame? But some mothers created this monster.

Uniquely, it is common to hear this saying when people are complaining about the bride in a marriage; "when a wife pleases the husband, whatever complaints made against her by anyone is a waste of time". Truly there is nothing you do in life without some people condemning it. Some people just believe they are okay and any other person is not. As long as you derive satisfaction from what you have let them say. The complainant must complain and the listener must listen. Some people are just fastidious. You cannot please them.

This goes to prove right the saying that, "if a man marries an ugly wife and lives happily with her, with time people will begin to see beauty in ugliness". Character is the most important element in a woman the proverb still maintains. Beauty is not food. The bible says it is better to live at a roof top than to live with a contentious woman.

"A man's debt to his father in-law can never be fully paid." Marriage is a continuous thing. Immediately a marriage is contracted, a lifelong relationship has been established. Your in-law becomes your brother and vice-versa. Although with increase in divorce in our society, the marriage institution is greatly threatened. That closeness and lifelong ties are being broken.

For those who have decided to keep their marriage, there is no sacrifice made to one another that is too much. A man who decides to give the daughter out to another man has bestowed trust in that man. And the one who decides to marry another man's daughter has shown he is reliable.

On a broader spectrum, there are people who are very nice to us in life. We are indebted to them either in kind or cash and there is nothing we can present that can equate our regards for such people.

Salt is supposed to maintain its saltiness. Once it loses it, it is no more regarded as salt. Similarly, a married woman is expected to behave as being married. For a woman to be married means she is no more a baby. It is a mark of maturity. Hence, the saying that "when a woman passes the phase when it is no more asked whose daughter is this, she enters whose wife is this? "That proverb reveals that life is graduated and people observe us and questions are asked. If you are not at the phase you are supposed to be, something is lacking. It brings shame and dishonour most times. Like the bible pointed out in Ecclesiastes 3, there is time for everything.

Sometimes when separated or divorced couples are asked why their marriage hit the rock, they will tell you they discovered they were incompatible and decided to split. This proverb may be instructive to such persons. Our elders say: "If a man sought for a companion who acted like him, he would live in solitude."* No two people can be the same. Marriage is about how you handle your incompatibility. If you are already compatible with your spouse, there is no need for a marriage.

What makes marriage interesting is our ability to harness our differences, idiosyncrasies, and weakness towards advancing a cause. The strength of the man may help the weakness of the woman and vice-versa. Have we bothered to find out why some men don't ever make progress in life until they get married? Some men need the aura of their wife to brighten theirs before they can make progress in life. This may look like a mystery. But not all things can be explained.

It is also funny when some men think that they are being manly when they beat up and brutalise their wife. An adage says: "it is not bravery for a man to beat his wife". Our wives are better half to us. When you brutalise your wife, you are brutalizing yourself. Both of you are supposed to be one. It is said that "when the eyes start shedding tears, the nose starts running". In fact, the bible says that one of the ways a man's heavens can be opened is when that man loves his wife. For a man that brutalizes his own, the heaven may be sealed with steel. You can then imagine his predicament.

"Never make an early morning appointment with a newly married man" our people said. It is obvious that a newly married man has a business at hand. He needs to ravish the wife and the wife needs his warmth and comfort. It would be foolhardy for anyone to think that he can break this natural tie. Generally, it does not make sense going into an agreement you know too well that cannot be honoured. By virtue of some people's situation and circumstances, it is obvious that they may not be able to abide by certain agreements.

"When a woman calls the husband a useless man, that relationship is at the labyrinth of collapsing." There are certain checks in marriages or relationships which serve as thermometer reading to find out the true health of the relationship. When certain level is exceeded, know that the relationship is beyond repairs. It is like when handshake goes beyond the elbow, it turns into another thing.

This is because out of the abundance of the heart the mouth speaks. The thought before a man was killed wasn't spontaneous. It must have been considered many nights before the actual act. The relationship must have passed the rubicon of destruction.

However, when a woman understands the spouse very well and both of them live happily, the tendency is for the ignorant minds to conclude that the man had eaten love portion from the wife. Many people expect couples to always quarrel. Some will tell you that if a couple have not quarreled in a marriage know that the relationship is doomed. It is the devil's strategy to ensure that people don't enjoy marriage. Marriage is meant to be enjoyed and not endured.

It takes careful studying, patience and understanding for a couple to live in peace. These are people from different orientations, experiences and background. Like the bible says; a wise woman builds her home.

When you are building, it takes a lot of strength, energy, perseverance and planning; nothing good comes on a platter of gold. And every battle is won before going to the battle field.

"Adultery is not just about who you lie with, it is about who you lied to "** This saying expose in depth the dangers of adultery which is destroying the marriage institution today. Like the saying goes "it takes lies to make a lie, lie" Before adultery is committed, several lies must have been told. A survey conducted in the US said that about 47 percent of all married men have committed adultery while 35 percent of the females have had flings with another man. These figures may be conservative if we consider the alarming cases of marriage breakdown seen in our societies today.

Adultery is one sin the bible made us to understand that we commit with both our body and heart. Nobody just commits adultery in a jiffy. It takes a lot of scheming and thoughts. Our conscience tells us before the actual act is done, that what we are about to do is ungodly. But because we have allowed our inordinate desire to over shadow our sense of wellbeing, we fall for the sin only to realize it immediately the ephemeral happiness is over.

A man said that "he is not bothered that another man slept with the wife. Rather, he is concerned by what was said before and during the act". "No evil plan is executed on the spur of the moment. There are a lot of maneuvering done. Many things that are not supposed to be said are said. Many lies and aspersions are cast just because of material gains. No wonder Aristotle said that man's goal is the cause of crime.

....

A man said he is not bothered that
someone else slept with the wife
but he is bothered by what was
said before they slept together

....

Chapter Six

DEATH

THERE ARE THREE IDENTIFIED IMPORTANT events in the life of every human being. They are birth, marriage, and death. The events are celebrated in African societies. Most times an individual does not have control of what happens at his birth and death. But he has a significant decision to make during his marriage.

Consequently, many ceremonies are organized to celebrate these important events as ways of stressing their importance to the society. The events are like the biblical trinity which most Christians believe in. In fact, it is said that whenever a man is traveling and approaches a forked road, it serves as a reminder to the importance of the three events mentioned above, in the journey of life.

Although it is said that an individual is conscious of one of the three important events, still not everyone witnesses marriage in his life time. Some people die before they get married. Such people never had the opportunity of taking the only decision that nature allows them out of the three. Yet there are others who do not believe in marriage and don't enjoy the benefits this great institution provides.

Proverbs expectedly have been coined with these events. We saw some of the proverbs associated with marriage in the previous chapter. Here we shall see some of them fashioned out of death.

For a child that dies prematurely, it is common to hear this proverb: "The mushroom that does not want to be uprooted should not spring up." Mushrooms are delicacies in Africa. Whenever they are uprooted, the owner wants to make proper use of them. The same thing applies to the arrival of a new born baby. He is cherished and nurtured. The parents do this with the hope that the baby will grow up to become a responsible member of the society where he becomes of great use to the people. For any that does not want to live to become a good member of the society it is better he were not born.

On the general scene, the proverb cautions people who do not want to be helpful to others not to be around them or be seen visible in their space. Part of the reasons we are called human beings is because when any of us is in need, there should be someone to help.

Although death is a period of sorrow and pain, it provides an opportunity for people to sit down and examine their lives. It is usually a period for self appraisal-for the living. Perhaps this is what informed the saying that "when we see a dead man lying in state, it is a reminder that one day we shall be in that state."

The mushroom that does not want to be uprooted should not spring up.

Truly, "death is an inevitability." It is a necessary end that will come when its appointed time was due. Bearing this in mind, it is important we prepare for it. This is one of the ways of removing the torment of death when it comes. But only very few percentage of people in the world really prepare for death. Others just believe that whenever the unwanted guest knocks at their door they will know what to say.

As Africans celebrate death, many events are usually lined up to honour a dead person. The importance of the dead person and the number of lives he affected while alive may determine the type of burial he will receive. The burial rites involve dances, acrobatics, songs, folklores, pantomime and reveling. Each of these occasions provides opportunities for the use of masquerades.

However, the story was told of a wealthy farmer who before he died advised that his only son should be educated in the Western form of education having witnessed a bit of it. When he died, his relations squandered all his resources on funeral ceremony that there was nothing more left to educate the son.

A lot of efforts have been made by mortals to appease death. Some of the names given by Africans to their children reflect such effort at appeasement. It is not uncommon for instance to find people bearing such names as *Onwubiko* (Death, we implore you), *Ikegwuonwu* (Death may you get tired) *Anikulapo* (*death is in my pocket*) - Can death be appeased? No! This informs the proverbial saying that "Nobody should forget death while making plans here on earth."

Contending with the inevitability and unpredictability of death is as challenging in the African society as elsewhere. The reality of death indeed finds ample expression in various names and sayings.

A common saying in this environment is that death is a thief. It strikes unannounced, when it is least expected. Death steals away life when it is sweetest to those who have them. This deep expression becomes at once a caution about life and provides food for thought for mortals. The message is that life is most unpredictable. The view is an amplification of the words in the book of Ecclesiastes, which profoundly expresses life as vanity upon vanity, and vexation of the spirit. The happiest moment in life can easily become the saddest. It is therefore, unwise to boast with life and earthly riches.

Death does attract elaborate ceremonies in the African culture, for instance, in the course of celebrating burials in some African cultures such as among the Yoruba, Ijaw and Igbo in Nigeria and the Akan in

Ghana, the bereaved, the extended families and well-wishers often adorn uniform dresses, a symbol of unity in adversity. The uniform also distinguishes the family from other mourners.

The burial cloth (Jiri mara in Igbo and Asoebi in Yoruba) atimes tell stories on their own. The quality of the cloth tells the financial strength of the bereaved family. But most importantly, the design mortifies communicate a lot of information for the people. Some of them have ladder or staircase design pattern. This pattern traces its origin to the proverb: "One person alone does not climb the ladder of death."

> ***One person alone does not
> climb the ladder of death.***

This on its own is very instructive. Death is what is awaiting every mortal. No matter how big, small, powerful, or powerless, one day every mortal takes his turn in answering that nonnegotiable call of nature. What matters then is the work and legacy left behind, the number of lives we touched positively while alive. For life is not about how long one lived but how well. It is said of death also that it is like rain that does not fall on one roof. "Death does not dwell at a place". It moves to and from seeking for whom it may devour.

Remarkably "death does not have friend." No matter

what any one does, when death knocks at his door, he cannot escape. We can run but we can't hide from the claws of death. In life we can parley with our friend and he can spare us when we go astray. There is even room to demand for postponed judgement. However, when death knocks on anyone's door, there is no hiding place.

This proverb lies in tandem with another saying that: "Death does not know who is a king". It is a leveler. Although the rich might try to delay their death through good diet, exercise, and medical treatment, when the time is up there is no escape. A lot of them have joined one clandestine body or the other. This has not provided solution to death. Rather, it has worsened it. The more people try to run away from death, the nearer they draw to it. The best approach is to recognize it and live a godly, righteous and sober life here.

For those who have decided to take their fate philosophically the next proverb strengthens their belief. "Death meant for all does not elicit fear." In life, whatever we cannot change we should ask God for the courage to bear it. Since death is inevitable, there is no need dreading it. Instead, we should be preparing for it daily, bearing in mind that it can strike at any time.

As a way of alleviating the sorrow of death on many African societies there is the saying that "Life is a market place, when you are through with buying or selling you go." Truly if people can understand that this world is not our home as Jim Reeves the gospel musician pointed out several years ago, then we will all make good effort to prepare for going home. But many people have made the earth their home. For such people everything ends here on earth. There is no life after death. If our hope ends on this earth, we are miserable.

Death however is not all about evil and sorrow. It humbles us and brings out the human in us. If there was nothing like death, this world would have been a very terrible place. Death brings some sanity into the earth.

Alfred Nobel, the Swedish chemist who made fame and fortune by inventing the dynamite and licensing the formula to many governments for the manufacture of explosives and weapons of war was lucky to read his obituary while alive. When his younger brother died, a newspaper mistakenly thought he was the one and printed a powerful editorial paying tribute to him. In the article, Alfred Nobel was remembered as the inventor of the dynamite and it concluded thus: "He was a man who made fortune by enabling armies to achieve new levels of mass destruction".

Nobel was shocked with the editorial, that he will be remembered when he dies for inventing Weapons of Mass Destruction (WMD). He quickly formed a trust for search for peace and achievements in different fields of human endeavours. Today Alfred Nobel is only remembered for instituting the Nobel Prize recognized globally for the search for peace and advancement in research into different fields of human knowledge. What an irony? But it was only made possible by that obituary he read about himself.

"Death does not book appointment." It happens at any time. This is where the motto of the Scout Movement is classical - "Be Prepared". At my secondary school, the prestigious Government Comprehensive, Borokiri, Port Harcourt, Nigeria, the motto of the institution is "Semper Paratus", two latin words that mean "Ever Ready". Those days any teacher in the all boys school can walk into a classroom and set a test for the pupils. If any of the students dare to complain, he would be reminded of the school's motto. This development later became a subtle oath any child admitted into the institution has taken to guide his life. This has worked wonders for many of the graduates of the school in their post secondary life.

Such mutual understanding helped the students a lot because everyone was mindful that he can be tested anytime. Therefore, hard work was the order of the day. Every student put his academic work before any other thing. The result then was that the school was always coming top in the state at any West Africa General Schools Certificate examinations. It would be nice if we can prepare on the daily basis to meet our maker.

Jesus Christ, while carrying out his ministry here on earth advised his disciples to be prepared always. He told them and by extension all of us alive now not to build our treasures on earth where moth can devour them. The life we live today is like the children play; "Now you see me, now you don't". Life is like a shadow that vanishes away. It is like a vapour that evaporates.

Some people still behave as if the world belongs to them. They arrogate to themselves the title of alpha and omega. They forgot the saying that "A man who have never submitted to anything will soon submit to the burial mat." This proverb stresses the fact that all our victories or successes will be left behind one day when death comes knocking.

Jesus Christ, the second Adam is the only person who conquered death. He was crucified, he died and was buried. On the third day he resurrected after defeating death.

Today he is seated at the right hand of God almighty from where he intercedes for us daily. And without that singular act, every hope of all Christians would have been in vain. The monster (death) the bible tells us will be arrested at the close of the age and thrown into the fire that burns with sulphur.

To still stress the inevitability of death on the planet earth, our elders say "it is a promise everybody has made." When you make a promise, it is honourable to redeem it. Even if you forget, you will be reminded. If you escape redeeming any other vow, not that of death. When death comes, it is all obvious and consuming that there is no escape except in Jesus Christ. This is because the righteous don't 'die' they go to heaven. When we know we have a promise to fulfill, we prepare for it. Unfortunately, many men are so preoccupied with the cares of this world that they have become like the proverbial man who was busy chasing rats while his house was gutted down by fire.

But as consuming as death is, it is believed that it cannot be responsible for the extermination of any kindred or race. This is illustrated in this proverb.

"Death does not exterminate a clan but foolishness does." Foolishness is to be feared more than death. Death is not really responsible for people's death. It emerges at the final scene to play its role of ending the game. Foolishness kills. It is foolishness that will make a man commit grave mistake. And every mistake has a consequence. We are in a world of cause and effect. Some mistakes can be rectified while some are irreparable. Man has to be careful. No wonder the bible says it is not expected of man to take charge of the affairs of his life. Man by nature is fallible.

Many people who are dead today died as a result of one costly mistake or the other which was as a result of their foolishness. The bible says a fool calls sin enjoyment. Fancy this scenario, many people engage in many acts that are contrary to the will of God and when they are advised they say you are infringing on their right to liberty or enjoyment. Is this not foolishness?

Because death is the period when people are in pain and grief, it is difficult for anybody to forgive any person who was in the position to sympathize with them when they were bereaved but chose to do other things. This informed the saying that: "It is better to go to where people are mourning than where they are making merry." Death is a period of self-examination.

There is a lot to learn. Sometimes, we have cathartic expiation that purges us of excess emotion. Even the holy bible admonishes us to sympathise with those mourning, stressing that "it is better to be where people are mourning than where they are making Merry".

"We can only cure sickness and not death." This is a saying which informs us about the futility of any one trying to revive the dead. It is a general warning on those who would want to expend energy on worthless ventures. It does not pay. It makes no sense for anyone to wash his hands clean before cracking kernel for fowls. We all have to make hay while the sun shines.

....

***We can only cure sickness
and not death.***

....

Chapter Seven

PROVERBS THAT QUESTION

"**A** MAN WHO ASKS QUESTIONS DOES not miss his way" is a popular aphorism in Africa. Whatever you don't know is older than you" our people say. When you ask questions about anything you're ignorant about, you become enlightened and educated about it through the informed answers given by those knowledgeable on the subject. Asking question is a mark of humility and civilization. A proud mind feels he knows it all and can't condescend to ask others.

The result is that such person is made a fool. His actions reveal his ignorance. Like the proverbial saying that "When the mouth vomits, it reveals what it has eaten." When an ignorant man speaks in the public, he exposes his ignorance.

In the art of conversation, questioning is very important. Some questions in conversation come in the form of proverbs. They leave the person they are directed at gapping for answers if he were not wise. The ability to provide answers to proverbial questions would educate, enlighten, and entertain the people present.

When the mouth vomits, it reveals what it has eaten.

Sometimes the proverbial questions are ironical. It takes a man of wisdom to decode the message and respond effectively to its content. The inability to identify such ironical proverbs may result in wrong responses which may prove that the communication was ineffective and may not produce the desired result. It takes an understanding of the scenario of an interrogative proverb to make a meaning out of it. For example, there is a saying that "a man making love to a widow and fidgeting, does it mean he doesn't know where the husband had gone to?" A widow is a woman whose husband is dead. A man making love to her should not be afraid because the late husband cannot apprehend him. So, fidgeting does not make any sense. But the proverb is a query on the ability or qualification of anyone who is supposed to be carrying out a task with all the confidence yet he is afraid.

Equally, over indulgence in anything is bad. Life's best philosophy is moderation. When people indulge in extreme behaviour, that is when the society is at a risk. The proverb" the mother goat that delivers twin always, what is the state of the pelvic bone?", goes to express the ills of extremity. Anyone that over in dulges in anything will sooner or later wear himself out and the consequence of this is severe.

A good example of over indulgence is found amongst flirts or sex predators. Perhaps this gave rise to the saying that: "One shouldn't be carried away by the excitement sex gives in order not to kill the baby in the womb." Many people spoil their case because of lack of patience. Many have ruined their lives today because of Dutch-happiness they derive from certain activities.

We are aware of the increasing incidences of drug abuse in our society today. Many young men and women who had bright future had them shattered because of abuse of hard drugs. A lot of them are roaming the streets or are in rehabilitation clinics now. Instead of being assets to the society they are now liabilities.

In another vein, some people's problem is that they are just ungrateful. They can never appreciate any good thing done for them. They are always longing to be like another person. Not only are this type disgusted with themselves, they don't appreciate the good work God has done in them. Consequently, they developed low esteem. This peters out any good quality or feature they have.

Whatever you can change in life and have the means to do it, you can proceed with it. But when you are confronted with a situation you can't change, what do you do? You ask God to give you the grace to bear it. That is why it is asked proverbially: "If you tell a short man that he is short and he gets annoyed will he grow overnight?" Of course, the answer is no. He would have reached the point where he can't grow up again since he is now a man. He can only expand sideways.

When you find yourself in "I can't help it" situation, it is the best time to approach God for help. God works faster for us when our physical effort has failed us and we are able to recognize him as being able.

Thus, we can surrender ourselves to him. But when we can still help ourselves, we don't need God.

"When a Billy goat hides inside a room and the offensive odour fouls the outside, has it really hidden from the predators?" Of course the answer is no. Everyone can locate it by perceiving the awful odour. It is like the case of the ostrich that buries its head in the sand whenever there is an enemy.

This action is a show of stupidity. Many people engage in fruitless ventures and bank on mother luck to help them when it is obvious that they have failed right from the first step. Some go to the extent of having plastic surgery to change their looks. People still have vivid memory of who they are and can easily link them with their old image.

Some other people are known to pay their mentors in bad coins. In some extreme cases, some people have killed those who trained them or put them in positions of authority. This informed the maxim: "The man who killed the native doctor that prepares charm for him, does it mean all his enemies are dead? "What the man has succeeded in doing is making himself more vulnerable. He is like a city without a wall that can be attacked at any time.

When a man blocks his anus, he may not be able to pass faces again and may die of constipation. It does not pay anyone to cut off the nose to spite the face. And when the lizard abandons the iroko tree, its predator will quickly apprehend it.

Pretence and deceit are vices also condemned seriously in Africa. There are times people pretend so much that they piss off others. This proverb may do a lot of good in bringing such people back to the path of honour. "When a woman that claims she does not eat rat meat then shares it with her teeth amongst the children, has she not eaten from it?"

It is as clear as the crystal that the woman participated in eating a rat meat. Many people claim they don't eat or do certain things yet they still do them in other ways. Fancy somebody that claims to be a vegetarian eating egg. He has eaten meat of course. He may fool himself but he can't fool everybody.

This is a big hypocrisy and the person may be likened to the proverbial ostrich which hid the head inside sand when the predators approached nearer and thought she was out of their view. It is like when a man dives inside the bed of a river and the back is seen by people standing out. He has not hidden. He is still within the purview of public eyes.

And everybody has a gift which God the perfect creator bestowed each person with. Many call it talent. Others call it palm marks. Many have gone further to find out what their future holds for them. Some people call it destiny. No matter what name is given to it, the truth is that there is nobody God created without a talent.

Whereas some people have taken time to discover their talent, developed it and are making contributions positively to the world, others are busy blaming their stars and family background as being responsible. They forgot that between yesterday's lost opportunities and tomorrow's promises there is a gap, a today that is still full of blessings. Only those that have identified their destiny and are able to develop it, can benefit themselves and society with it.

It is said that "if the fowl leaves the chom, Chom sound it makes whilst in search for food for the chicks, how will it feed them?" If we abandon what God has blessed us with, we can't but be throwing aimless punches that do not bring any tangible thing in return. The bible says, "a man's gift makes a way for him. It is what God has blessed you with, that skill you have that will come to your rescue when the chips are down.

Sometimes we are in a hurry to do things. Because of this lack of patience to get things done properly, we make fatal mistakes which retard our progress. Patience is a virtue. The bible says which of us after being anxious can add or subtract a strand of hair from the head. Life is the most precious gift of God. It should be enjoyed.

We should not be in a hurry to go home but rather we should learn the art of coasting home like milers. Consequently, it is asked: "A man who hurriedly licked all his fingers after a meal, will he hang them on the rafters of a roof?"

This should be an advice to those who are always anxious or gregarious about life. Some people feel time is against them and that they have not achieved what they were supposed to achieve. One may be tempted to enquire from such people where they spent all their time. It is common seeing such persons trying to do many things at the same time without achieving any positive result. Their case becomes like that of the proverbial puppy that wanted to answer two calls at the same time and ended up breaking the jaw.

This reminds us of the statement credited to the first president of Nigeria Rt. Hon. (Dr)Nnamdi Azikiwe, and the Owelle of Onitsha who died at the age of ninety-four. Prior to his death, he was asked in a press interview about life after death. He responded that he was not in a hurry to leave the earth because he was not sure that life existed in another planet. And he really enjoyed life. About 10 years before he finally died it was announced on Nigeria's national Television network that he was dead. But the staunch politician outlived most of those behind his death hoax.

"A man whose wife delivered and he claims he was taken unawares does it mean nine months wasn't enough notice?" This saying is an advice to people who always claim that they were taken unawares by events that gave them warnings. Nine months are enough for the man to prepare for the wife's delivery. But lazy and indolent people will always adduce even the funniest excuse at any given time. It gives credence to the saying that if we fail to plan, we have already planned to fail.

Some people say there is nothing like coincidences in life. Everything has been planned from the beginning of creation. Such view has a big support in the Yoruba proverb which says: "A witch cried in the night and the little baby died in the morning, there must be a link between the two events."

Truly witches are real and they don't cry in vain. They are always out to wreck havoc on people. The bible says a thief comes to kill, to steal and to destroy. A witch is a thief. It comes unannounced and it leaves scars of sorrows, tears and blood behind. It is not every happening in life that requires proof or alibi. But that does not negate their reality and existence.

The name of a certain market, in Imo state, South East Nigeria is Eke 'Nmegbuoha,' literally translated to the market where the public is cheated. There is a saying that "if a man attended Eke Nmegbuoha and returns home to complain that he was cheated does it mean he did not understand the meaning of the name before going to the market?"

Many of us are fore warned about dangers ahead but most times we choose to ignore the warning until when we come face to face with the problem. The name of the market was an enough caveat emptor for the man. But he preferred trying his luck. As another saying goes "anybody killed by a train is deaf." Whoever falls victim of a trap after being warned is either cursed or destined to suffer that way.

George Bernard Shaw, the Nobel laureate for literature, a playwright and dramatist in his play Saint Joan posed this proverbial question: "Must a Christ die in every generation for those who have no imaginations." Many people are wandering from pillar to post seeking for help when help is at their door step. They become the man said to have eyes but can't see. Have ears but cannot hear.

Another way of this is the saying that. "When we hear a house has fallen do we ask if the ceiling fell with it?" It would be stupid for anyone to ask such a question. When a house caves in, the ceiling must surely collapse with it. Some people get deluded in life thinking that something can still be saved out of a hopeless situation. Except the person is a student of faith, his waiting is tantamount to waiting for Godot in Samuel Beckett's absurd play.

No matter how devilish a man may be, it is believed in Africa that he owes his son the truth. Hence these proverbs "Can any sane man send his son with a potsherd to a neighbour's hut to bring fire and turn round to send rain to him?" Or "has it ever been heard that a child was scolded by the piece of yam his mother put in his palm?". These are sayings to buttress that nobody in his right senses would want to wish evil to his loved one not to talk of unleashing it.

When a parent goes out of this belief as we often

see sometimes with mother's who murder their little children or husbands who kill their wives and vice-versa, we know it is more than meets the eyes. Love does not hate. When we love somebody, we wouldn't want to harm the person.

In another pedestal, we meet fastidious people as we go about our daily businesses. Some are not only fastidious but greedy and insatiable in their demands. A roommate in the University used to ask that: "If a man visits his house and ate seven pieces of yam and complains of having tooth ache when his tooth is good, will he eat a human being?"

Put differently, our elders say, "If a chicken that ate corn, drank water, swallowed pebbles suddenly complained of not having teeth, if it developed teeth, will it eat a man?"

This reminds me of an incident as an undergraduate student. During the rainy semester holiday after my second year, one of my cousins' new girl friend visited. As it was our custom when guests come, he enquired from her if she would like to have a drink served her. The lady said no. My cousin wanting to impress his new catch, pressurised her to have a drink. But she insisted that she wouldn't. On the third account, the lady accepted to have a drink. My cousin requested to know her brand. She said: "Okay could you serve me one big bottle of Guinness stout beer for a start." My cousin was shocked. The question now is, if she is starting with a big bottle of Guinness stout beer, by the time she was done, she would have consumed 6 big bottles. The consequences of this on herself and my hapless student cousin's pocket will not be a child's place. Before he could say Jesus is Lord, the girl has gulped it. Nobody bothered to ask her if she needed another. Action, they say speaks louder than words.

My cousin did not need a soothsayer to tell him that such a girl is dangerous. She might be insatiable both materially and otherwise. After that day, we did not take the risk of looking for the girl.

Our elders say "when handshake passes the elbow it has turned into another thing". And "when sleep passes two market days it becomes death and no longer sleep".

And when you see a man who is so stingy that he can't offer himself a treat, it is better to keep him at arm's length. Nothing good can come out of such person.

You have to love yourself before loving others. This confirms the saying that "when crocodiles eat their own eggs, what will they not do to the flesh of a frog. "When somebody shows a lot of meanness to himself, is it you an outsider he will show kindness?

Similarly, "no matter how long the wooden boat stays in the river, does that make it a crocodile?" No! Many people try to claim what they are not. But that does not make them that thing they claim. They are only deluding themselves. For instance, a lady who decides to bleach the skin because she wants to be accepted as white, it's all waste of time. What makes one white is not on the skin pigment. There are many other important criteria to identify one as white.

After all, the hood does not make the monk. What makes up a human being is not the physical look but the spiritual. That which the eye can see is ephemeral and perishable but that we can't see is eternal and the most valuable assets in life.

Therefore, it is a type of illusion for someone to claim what he is not. Like the saying goes that "when the wind blows we shall see the rump of the fowl". Put differently, "when the wind blows, we shall know that Catholic church priests also wear trousers".

"Is it possible for a cockroach to be safe in the mist of fowls?" This proverb is akin to the former. Cockroaches and fowls are never friends. Cockroach is food for the fowl and no fowl spears it. It will be foolhardy for any cockroach to pretend to be having a nice time where fowls are.

When a man tries to be a friend to his enemy, his days are numbered. Nobody sees a danger and decides to plunge into it. Rather you do all within your power to avoid such danger. It reminds us the story of a white garment prophet who wanted to re-enact the scene of the biblical Daniel in the Lions' den. Whereas the biblical Daniel was thrown into the Lions' den because he refused to worship a graven image, the Daniel at Ibadan went to the University of Ibadan zoological garden to test his magical power.

No sooner had he jumped into the lion's cage without permission than the hungry lion perhaps starved for some time because of dearth of funds for the zoo, pounced on the false prophet and tore him into pieces.

He wanted glory for himself and since God cannot share his glory with an ordinary mortal, he was devoured by the lion.

··

**When breeze blows we shall
see the rump of the fowl.**

··

Chapter Eight

WOMEN IN PROVERBS (WIP)

"**A** WOMAN WHO TELLS THE HUSBAND every happening around is never hated" is a popular African proverb. In Africa polygamy was very rampant. But Christian belief, modernisation and perhaps hardship are ameliorating the extent of polygamy practice currently. It is easy now to find many men sticking to only one wife until death do them part. It is different from the past when a man's wealth was measured by the number of wives he married and children he brought forth into the world.

There are instances where some men married more than 50 wives. As outrageous as this might be, the record set by King Solomon of old who married 700 wives and had 300 concubines remains to be broken. It is important to stress here that King Solomon's era and our present generation is not the same. Apart from that, God blessed King Solomon with uncommon wisdom and material wealth which were very important in managing the harem of wives and concubines he had.

> *A woman who tells the*
> *husband every happening*
> *around is never hated.*

Most of those who marry many wives now are just gluttonous of the female folks. What follows accumulation of women is unhealthy rivalry. Each of the women would want to out maneuver the other. Every obnoxious means is applied. After all, in warfare all is fair. Gossip is a big tool in this kind of situation. A woman that is adept in gossip and maneuvering gains the upper hand. She is always quick to see, hear and speak and she gains more attention from the husband.

The same thing happens in the larger society. Most rich men love gossips. They always cherish people who tell them what people say and feel about them. They shower such people who gossip to them with gifts. And to continue to gain recognition, the gossip designs all sorts of obnoxious means to gather information and equally report to his rich boss.

Nothing lasts forever. There is a time for everything

on earth. A good understanding of this fact will make us appreciate life the more and also live positive and quality lives. Perhaps this informed the reason why a woman who is in her late 20s and there is no suitor and not in a serious relationship, she becomes apprehensive.

Viewed literally, we know how many flowers that blossomed with the rise of the sun also shrunk with the scotch of heat in the afternoon. Similarly, we see many women who appeared very beautiful yesterday and today their beauty has petered out. Perhaps that is why when a woman is in her late teens or twenties and no suitor is coming her way, she gets apprehensive because she knows her days to shine are numbered.

Furthermore, this development led to another saying that "When a married woman starts aging, it appears as if the husband never paid any bride price on her". Really when things get old, they appear to lose value. Sometimes we wonder if actually they cost us something.

For instance, bride price is usually paid on a woman before she gets married. What may encourage any man to make such payment could be the beauty of the woman he saw. If the way some women appear at old age was how they were at the point of marriage, many men would have loved to stay single. This is because the magnetic field that pulled them to the women is now lacking.

The two proverbs above could be interpreted to mean the transient nature of life. Nothing lasts for long. Therefore, nobody should boast with the things of this world. They are good and blossoming today, tomorrow they wither out. We can only remember them by the memory they left in our brains.

Yet another proverbial saying sees "a woman to be like a cloth in a market place." A cloth in the market is always given to the highest bidder. The man who offers the highest takes her. There is no morality in business. But this saying may not always be true because these days some women reject men of stupendous wealth for young men with bright future. Others that are wealthy prefer marrying young men they can control.

A kind hearted woman is said to be easily insulted by the husband's relations. Most time people mistake some people's kind disposition to stupidity and insult them. When some people try to be nice to others, it is easily abused. No wonder it is said that "the good ruler who stands for the people becomes a victim too soon. But a bad ruler like bad sauce, stays longer."

When people see those, they can beat up, they are quick to challenge them to a fight. When the reverse is the case, they adduce all sorts of excuses. This proverb that "when a nursing mother sees another woman she can beat up, she quickly drops her baby to attack her. But when she sees another who can beat her, she will use her baby as an excuse" suffices.

Our elders say "Woman with a big buttocks may not know that she is carrying a heavy load until there's an emergency that mandates her to run for dear life". For instance, many people are being advised to lose weight because of the health implications of overweight. But only few people comply to this advice. Others are waiting for when they are caught up with the problems and they will be running from pillar to post asking for solutions.

A woman that sells 'ogiri' (a type of food spice made of fermented pumpkin seeds) can accurately identify a house fly that is blind. The ogiri spice gives a kind of awful odour that attracts so many flies around the seller. The proverb attests to the fact that those who are adept at doing certain things can easily distinguish the different happenings around. They can tell you in the minutest details what are involved in what they do.

It is often said that "there is no how you will wash an old woman's cloth without discovering some particles of faeces." There are situations in life we can't find lasting solutions for no matter how much we try. Old age is natural. It has a time it comes in everybody's life. Nature has made some situations as they are and any attempt to change them may be counter-productive.

It further goes to buttress how fastidious some people can be, no matter the good you have done for them, they are never satisfied. You may use this proverb to stress such situations. Perhaps this saying below may strengthen the one above. "When dry bones are mentioned in a proverb, an old woman becomes edgy." There are ugly situations many people find themselves. Some of the situations are caused by them while others are un-explainable or caused by other people to them. So, whenever such situations are mentioned or touched in their life, it affects the soul of their life. Many would wish such situations could just vanish with a blink of an eye. If wishes were horses beggars would ride.

For the women who prove stubborn before the male folks, this saying is for them. "A woman who is proving stubborn to a man will she make love to herself?" In Africa, the female folks, it is believed should be seen but not heard. It is almost an abomination or as a friend jokingly put it, it is an 'abomi-continent' for a woman to challenge a man.

This development may anger many women in the Western hemisphere and they may call us uncivilized or barbaric. It may also make champions of gender equality mad with anger, making the resolutions of the famous Beijing, China and other female conferences on gender equality bunkum. But that is the true position in Africa. It is not something to be Wished away. It is part of the culture there. Perhaps this is part of those things that made African culture different from the west. Of course, the world would have been too monotonous and dull without cultural differences like this.

A woman who is proving stubborn to a man will she make love to herself?

The saying is a lesson also for people who feel they are an Island and do not need other people. We need each other in our daily endeavours. Men and women, children, and adult, white or black, tall, or short, educated and illiterate are all needed-for our world to be a better place. None should see himself as indispensable as nobody can clap with one hand.

Beyond this, "a woman cannot place more than the length of her leg on her husband" our people say. It is what anyone has in life that he can offer to others. When you observe somebody offering what he does not have perhaps in attempt to please others, it is either he has started stealing or robbing Peter to pay Paul. And he who robs Peter to pay Paul must always count on Paul for support and of course the centre cannot hold.

Chapter Nine

PATIENCE

AN ADVERTISEMENT BILL BOARD MESSAGE on property development in Nigeria had these wordings "A patient dog eats no bone". The advertisement was very creative. It arrested people's attention. Before long it became a popular slogan in the commercial centre of Nigeria-Lagos. The bill board message reminded many of the ancient proverb. "A patient dog eats the fattest bone". But this time the opposite was being emphasized.

Advertising allows free use of phrases and words. It even allows copying. Advertisers like journalists have poetic license. They can turn any phrase, word, or sentence to suit their own purpose.

There is however, no doubting the old maxim that a patient dog eats the fattest bone. It is a wise saying that has withstood the test of time. Patience is an indispensable aspect of our life. Anyone that lacks it can as well leave the planet earth because we all need it at different times of life to stay alive. It sustains hope.

And hope helps keep the light of life aglow. No wonder the bible says: "Patience is a virtue." It is a good quality of life every human being must possess.

There is no aspect of our life we do not need patience. What makes it possible for anyone to receive that which he was promised that has not materialised is Patience. It is a brother of faith. Without patience no two people can live together. And the world would have been a very miserable place to live in.

It is said that "A penis that did not die young will eat a bearded meat". This adage rekindles patience and encourages hard work. Though the tone appears vulgar, like it was pointed out earlier on, proverbs are no respecter of persons. What is important is the message that is being conveyed.

Looked at literally, when a male child is born, he has a penis that is used at that stage for urinating and not reproduction. He is not expected to engage in any sexual act at that age." "It is a taboo for a little child to do that. It is legally and morally wrong for him to be engaged in sex at that age. When he grows into adulthood, he is legally allowed to do it. But it must be with a consenting adult. The bearded meat represents what is good and matured.

Broadly viewed, the proverb elucidates the importance of waiting for the right atmosphere or thing to emerge. Many people are too impatient and because of this, they miss what rightly belongs to them. For example, there are cases of men who refused to wait for their right future partners. At the end, they discovered that they were infatuated and then it was already late.

*****

A penis that did not die young will eat a bearded meat.

*****

Patience is even a mark of obedience. Any man that lacks patience cannot be obedient to any cause. If anyone is not obedient, he can't achieve anything in life. The bible enjoined us that if we are faithful and obedient, we will eat the good of the land.

"It is with good tongue that the snail uses to crawl on thorny sticks". The snail is already a slow animal. In fact, to say that a human being has a snail spirit is to say he is unprogressive. But in this slow movement, the snail comes across thorny objects yet it navigates through them and continues its journey.

The proverb advises us that no matter how bad a situation might be, how we comport and carry our-selves will determine the success we can achieve. There are so many people who give in immediately they encounter any obstacle on their way. They think that the journey of life is very smooth. No good thing comes so cheaply. If you want gold, you must dig deep enough. And even when you find the raw gold, it must be tested in the fire for it to be refined and become pure gold. So, there is no means adopted to get gold that is cheap. That accounts for why gold is an expensive product.

Quitters it is said don't win a race. And winners don't quit. Most of the good things we are enjoying today like scientific and technological breakthroughs were achieved after several years of failures and huge resources expended. Yet the researchers were not discouraged. They did not abandon them. Today our world is far better than it was before.

Even the ants exercise a lot of patience perhaps we have a lot to learn from the bed bugs. "Mother bed-bug advised the little ones not to be bothered by the intense heat they are passing through because what is hot will surely be cold later." With patience we could overcome even the worst situations in life. This proverb even reminds us of the popular saying that "whatever that goes up must come down except our ages."

All that we need most in every bad situation we find ourselves is to be patient and back it up with prayers. Prayers move mountains. But it is only a patient person that can pray. Nothing is constant except change. A situation cannot but get better. However, it takes only a patient person to enjoy the fruit of patience. For only those who run a race to the end win trophies.

Many people are known to have committed suicide when they were faced with unpleasant situations. Not only is suicide a cowardly act, such people forgot that their life does not belong to them and they will have to account for what they did with it at the end of the age. Suicide smacks of an absolute manifestation of ungodliness and total lack of patience.

The vulture is one other animal that is very patient. If it sights an animal being slaughtered or a decomposing corpse somewhere, the vulture will perch on nearby tree or rooftop of a house waiting patiently for the coast to be cleared for it to descend and devour the carcass left behind. This might take hours. This development gave rise to the saying that the vulture said "she will not lose hope of scavenging for food at the market square until 6:30pm."

From African time belt, by 6: 30p.m, it has started getting dark as the sun must have slacked. Most market women would have started going home. Then the vulture can descend and scout for its food which is mainly carcass of animals.

Similarly, it is said that "No matter how high the termite might fly, it will still fall on the ground for the frogs to prey on it." This piece of advice is to aid man, created in God's image who finds it very difficult to exercise patience. Sometimes we expend so much energy in different directions trying to fix things when we could have waited for the right time to acquire such things without much pains.

Lack of patience is the major cause of depression, confusion, strife and many societal ills that are prevalent now. Many families are at loggerhead today because of this problem. Many villages, towns and countries are at war due to lack of patience. The irony of it all is that before any war can be resolved the warring factions must exercise patience and come to the negotiation table. So, instead of the more expensive way of coming to the negotiation table after a war must have started, why not exercise patience, and keep negotiating.

Anyone that lacks patience and claims to be a child of God is deceiving himself. God is patient with us if not, none of us can be alive today. We who are made in the image of God are supposed to manifest that attribute of God.

Majority of the crashed marriages in our societies now are attributable to lack of patience. In fact, some spouses are not patient enough to listen to their partners' views or complaints whilst making decisions. There is a saying that "as the bitter kola sounds in the mouth when being chewed is not how it tastes. "Marriage is not all bed of roses. It is also bitter in as much as it is sweet. That is why makers of wedding cake add both honey and vinegar. The two ingredients symbolize the sweetness and bitterness of marriage. But every couple must strive so that the bitter aspect of the union is grossly minimized.

Equally too, there are times we run helter-skelter in search of solutions for our problems. In this search, we are beclouded by wrong vision. For in-stance, there are many couple confronted with the monster of infertility or barrenness. Instead of seeing a fertility expert and telling it to God in prayer since the bible made us to know that children are heritage from the Lord and that none of us shall be barren in our land not even our cattle, they start jumping from one fetish doctor or white garment prayer house to the other.

Consequently, those people compound the problem by giving them concoctions or making them believe that the cause of their problem is their mother or relation. Even when such people eventually give birth through that method, you may discover that the baby is already demonized because it must have been fetched from the mermaid. And "he who ate the scrotum of a ram is indebted to elephantiasis of the scrotum," an adage says.

As the bitter kola sounds in the mouth when being chewed is not how it tastes.

Chapter Ten

ANIMALS IN PROVERBS

ANIMALS PLAY SIGNIFICANT ROLES IN proverbial sayings in Africa. They also play important roles as resource materials for folktales, fables and storytelling in Africa. Many issues in proverbs are discussed using animals both domestic and wild as the dramatis personae. It is like the cartoon or puppet theatre where animals are extensively used in conveying messages to people.

Proverbs with animal characters are developed after careful and long observations of the behaviour and life styles of the various animals used. Some people are tempted to enquire sometimes when the animals used in a proverbial saying was seen saying things credited to them. But such questions may not get an immediate answer.

However, Eneke Ntioba the bird said "as men have learned to shoot without missing, it has also learnt to fly without perching", "This saying is a good example of one of Isaac Newton's laws of motions which says that "actions and reactions are equal and opposite". When a people or government makes new law or policy, those it will affect, also design a new strategy to survive it.

It has been observed that when new drugs are developed for a disease, sometimes the germ develops a new resistance. Put mildly, most times when a government introduces a new law, people either overtly or covertly try to develop a new resistance or approach to circumventing the law. It could be said to be natural.

And to express the importance of vouchsafing for only people we are sure of, listen to this proverb. "The monkey said it can only vouchsafe for the young ones in the womb and not those already delivered, she is not sure of their loyalty."

This saying serves as a caution to a lot of us who are quick to stand in for people we do not know. Even when we know them, we have to be sure we know their character and what they are capable of doing. As the English law expert Lord Alfred Denning once said "Even the devil cannot tell what is in a man's mind". The man you are vouchsafing for do you know his intentions?

Well, the dog says "if he falls for you and you fall for him is all love". Love is reciprocal. It takes two to tango, an English proverb says. If in any relationship one person is nurturing it, it will not last for long. The two parties must put in their best to ensure that the relationship works.

**_The monkey said she can only
vouchsafe for the children in the
womb as for those already delivered,
she is not sure of their loyalty._**

Furthermore, the dog says "it loves walking behind anyone with a protruding stomach because if the person doesn't defecate, he will vomit". This is like a catch-22 proverb though this time the outcome is expected to be positive. Head the dog gains, tail he gains. A dog eats both excreta and vomits. Broadly viewed, this proverb is mainly applied when you do not stand to lose anything in probably a business or agreement you want to enter into. It is a win-win situation and does not elicit fear.

The vulture also shares in the Catch-22-like proverb. The male vulture said that "it is not afraid of the outcome of the eggs laid by the female vulture when they are hatched". The reason being that if the eggs are hatched into young vultures it is good news and if they die whilst being hatched, it is also good because they will serve as food.

Perhaps the billy goat's experience and that of the antelope may teach us useful lessons. The Billy goat said that "what it heard during funeral of a man is not good news because when a funeral ceremony reaches its frenzy, demands are made that a Billy goat should be slaughtered".

Truly there are situations in life when unwholesome demand is made of your time, person or resources and you are not favourably disposed to let go but you may be helpless because of the bondage your cultural heritage places on you. Fancy the scene in Chinua Achebe's "Things fall apart" when the oracle of the land demanded that the time has come for Ikemefuna to be sacrificed to the gods. Though a lad brought as a ransom for a Kinsman's wife that was killed by a neighbouring village, but the boy had adapted and settled as a member of Okonkwo's family. Suddenly, the oracle demanded he should be killed. It was a painful decision to let go.

Similarly, the antelope said that "it does not blame the hunter that shot and killed it, rather it blames the person who pointed at it before the hunter shot". There are situations when you must have almost escaped from a punishment or being apprehended for a crime being committed and suddenly somebody exposes you. You may never forgive that person and will continue to blame him for your misfortune.

For people who venture into things without counting the cost, they should learn some words of wisdom from the ant which says: roasting it in the fire isn't a problem but bring it out of the fire is where the problem lies. Even the Holy Scripture admonishes us to count the cost of following Christ. This is a call for all to evaluate whatever venture they want to embark on whether it is worth all the effort.

The crab, (crustacean) has its own message for

mankind. "The crab advises that when joke gets to the point of tying back the hands it is no more interesting." Whenever an unfavourable policy or style is adopted in a game or business, those affected tend to back out. Everybody expects to be treated fairly in any event or game. When the rule of a game becomes slanted, it automatically attracts protest and withdrawal.

There is an oriental philosophy which believes in uselessness as a way of long life. The philosophy uses a particular weed known as Siam (Obiarakara in Igbo language) meaning stranger who lords it over others wherever it goes. The plant it is argued is economically unviable but it multiplies easily wherever it finds itself. Unknown to the exponents of this philosophy, the plant can be used in fighting desert encroachment in Africa and it is tackling it well. This goes to support the saying that no situation or person is completely useless. There is something good about each of us. We need to identify it and work on it for our good.

The tortoise appealed to the captor to drop it on the ground for some seconds. He obliged it during which the tortoise uprooted trees, scattered leaves and made a mess of the place. The captor on seeing what the tortoise displayed asked why it did that. The tortoise replied that "at least people who will visit the scene later will know that I did not just succumb to my captor. I put up some resistance".

When problems come as they must, we shouldn't give up and organise pity party for ourselves. We have to confront problems head on. The devil and his messengers do not understand gentility. It is only force they know. No wonder the bible says that since the time of John the Baptist the Kingdom of God suffers violence and the violent take it by force.

Beyond this, sometimes it is good to be heard no matter the situation as observed by the chick carried away by a hawk. It said "I am not crying because I want the kite to release me, rather, I want the world to hear my voice". Make yourself to be heard if not for anything else but for record purposes. You might get help or have your own part of a case heard.

For loud mouths who boast a lot, they better learn from the plight of the Woodpecker. The Woodpecker is a master carver of wood. In fact, the name is an allegory. The bird boasted that "when the father dies, it will carve the biggest tree trunk around to make a casket for him. Unfortunately, when the father died, it developed a big boil on the mouth." This is a big warning that nobody knows tomorrow except God and we must stop boasting of it. Man born of woman is not expected to take charge of the affairs of his life.

Some of the proverbs credited to the animals come in story form but the messages they convey are the most important things. For example the shrew taunted the mouse rhetorically saying "you are an adult but looking smallish, how do babies look in your clan?" The mouse replied it thus: "As you are alive and smelling awfully, how do corpses smell in your kingdom?"

Perhaps the warning issued by the rat to Scrotal elephantiasis may help drive home some messages in this direction. "The rat cautioned scrotal elephantiasis to desist from frightening it because it is not as big as the calabash it rips open in the kitchen. Some people who may not have seen where you exhibited strength may want to challenge you sometimes until they know what you are capable of doing.

In the same vein, the crab complained bitterly saying that "it is agonizing that after swimming the ocean and emerging unharmed, it foolishly drowned inside the pot soup of a woman". What an irony? Truly it is agonizing to observe when a man who fought big battles and emerged victorious suddenly succumbed to little pressures of life. This confirmed the saying that "the stick that pierces a man's eyes is usually little.

....

***And the crab complained bitterly
saying that "it pains her that
after swimming the ocean and
emerging victorious, it got drowned
inside a woman's pot of soup".***

....

Sometimes we may have to congratulate ourselves when nobody deems it right to do it, after we are convinced, we have put up a good effort or fight. The lizard that fell from the big iroko tree looked around and no one applauded it, it nodded its head and said "since no one has congratulated me for the feat, I will congratulate myself. Jumping down from an iroko tree is not a joke. Anyone that thinks otherwise should make an attempt of doing it. The proverb goes to suggest that we must all be proud of our achievements.

Many people will stop at nothing to see that they never suffered from public disgrace or insult. This group of people may be likened to the "iji mbe" (a type of tiny flies that flock around people's head in the dry season) which says "instead it will receive insults from people, let its entire race be exterminated". No wonder, the more the flies are being killed, the more they perch around the head of their victims. This reminds us of the American boxer, Marvin Hagler credited for the saying in boxing "no retreat, no surrender". The boxer was famous for always advancing forward to punch the opponent whether he was losing or not.

Beyond this, not recognising some people's contributions in community building is causing some social upheaval. This may be one of the signs of egocentrism consuming our world in this generation. The frog has an advice for our society. It said "you can only know its true length upon its death". Truly when a frog dies, both the fore and hind limbs stretch out frontally and backwards. The is different from when alive during which both fore and hind limbs were folded to support its balance and movement on the ground. The message in this proverb is that we may likely know the importance of some people when they are no more with us Truly, the frog gets longer when she is dead. The legs and hands stretch out above her original length. The proverb reminds us that we may likely know the importance of some people when they are no more around.

Such persons' contributions may be recognised when their successors are not as knowledgeable or efficient when compared with them.

And no good thing comes on a platter of gold. If anyone doubts the claim above let him enquire from the Gorilla which said "fire is very beautiful to look at but it doesn't let people to cuddle it". As funny as this proverb may appear, you will accept that when we look at a blazing fire, the tongues appear beautiful but you can't draw nearer to it because it's very dangerous and deadly. This could also mean that most good things appear inform of problems, only those ready to brave the odds and confront them are successful.

But the irony of it all is that we all love beautiful things. There is a populist saying that "there is no body that spits out sugar put in his mouth. The quest for beautiful things have put many into trouble. It is common in marriages. Many men are carried away by the physical beauty of some women while some women are overwhelmed when they see men of wealth.

Appearance is not reality. What makes up a human being is on the inside and not out. The outside facade is very deceptive. The being is the part of man that relates with God. That should be what we all should be looking out for, the innate qualities in people and not carried away by deceptive outward looks.

Nevertheless, the sheep it was said told the dog

that "what you saw and has been barking, I have seen it long ago and maintained my cool". Some people are very good at advertising their problems or successes. There is every need for us to maintain some decorum when we are challenged or have achieved some success.

The sheep told the dog that "what he saw and was barking she has seen it a long time ago and kept quiet".

It is even more pronounced when somebody starts making wealth. Instead of allowing people to see the wealth by what he does, he goes about bragging and drumming it loud for people to hear.

However, it is said that "a well travelled youngster is more knowledgeable than a grey haired elder in the village". This is to attest that travelling has a lot of benefits. Travelling is education. It exposes the traveller to different cultures and traditions. Perhaps this is why the young Billy goat said that "had he not lived in his maternal home, he wouldn't have known how to stick up the mouth".

Chapter Eleven

WEALTH

IT SEEMS THAT THE POPULAR philosophy now is: 'Seek ye first the kingdom of wealth (money) and its power and every other thing shall be added unto you'. The quest for money has become so strong now than ever in most African societies that some people are ready to do anything to make it either hook or crook but mostly, the latter.

There are so many unthinkable ways people have adopted just to make money. For instance, there is increase in hard drug peddling, pornography, human trafficking, ritual murders and advanced fee fraud popularly known in Nigeria as 419. There is also an increase in armed robbery, pen robbery, bribery, and corruption, you just name it.

This drive is fired by the proverb that "wealth is strength". Therefore, people do not mind what it costs them to make it. And the society has stopped finding out people's source of wealth. All everybody is concerned in Africa is to be a partaker of every wealth. They have forgotten the old adage that "not enquiring about the source of any food offered to you before eating kills."

Wealth is strength.

In fact, many parents encourage their children to go to the cities and join their mates in doing whatever they are doing. The era where parents advise their children not to join others in doing evil is gone. When a child refuses to listen to their taunting to join their mates in the city, they label him as lazy and never do well.

Expectedly, those who made money through obnoxious means are now elevated into high positions. A lot of them are bestowed with chieftaincy titles while many have 'streets or monuments named after them. Of course, most of the people in this business never went to higher school. And the trend is making nonsense of formal education.

The society is suffering from it. Education enrolment is falling every year. Knowledge is now weakness. But they forgot that no society becomes important and developed without knowledge. It is knowledge that created money everybody is scrambling for.

Like Ecclesiastes says in chapter 5 vs. 10-11; Those

who love money will never have enough. How absurd, to think that wealth brings true happiness! The more you have, the more people come to help you spend it. So, what is the advantage of wealth, except perhaps to watch it run through your fingers."

Furthermore verse 15 says: "people who live only for wealth come to the end of their lives as naked and empty handed as on the day they were born."

We came empty handed into this world, we must leave empty handed. So, why do we kill ourselves in the name of acquiring wealth.

Perhaps we might learn a lesson from the saying: that "Wealth does not prevent death." No matter what we have, when death knocks, we must abandon them all to answer the supreme and last call. Many rich people are known to have wept while dying. May be because they were thinking of all the good things they are going to leave behind.

It is even worse when the wealth is ill-gotten. Jeremiah 17 v. 11 says; like a bird that hatches eggs she has not laid, so are those who get their wealth by unjust means. Sooner or later, they will lose their riches and at the end of their lives become poor old fools.

Truly many families where wealth was acquired illegally, soon become theatres of war when the 'bread winner' is no more. How to share the wealth becomes a big headache. Of course, lawyers and sycophants who never knew how the wealth was made make a lot of money from them through endless litigations both in the native and government courts.

Moreso, it can now be revealed why the rich is

always security conscious. Somebody that walks freely and aimlessly with you today, immediately he makes money, he surrounds himself with different security gadgets and personnels. It is often said that "when a man makes wealth and refuses to protect himself, he makes it possible for his adversaries to profiteer from his effort."

The only security (assurance) anybody should aspire to have should be in God. We know of many people who fortified themselves after making money yet their enemies still killed them. It is only in God we can boast of that surely no evil shall befall us. But it must be with the proviso that the wealth was rightly made and blessed by God. For he who goes to equity the lawyers say must go with a clean hand.

It is said however that in order to know a rich nation, you calculate its gross National Income and divide it by the population of the people. Therefore, in a village where there is one rich person, can that person truly claim he is rich? This informed the saying that "the wealth made by one man is no wealth".

This is because the person will be over burdened by demands the people around him will make of him. If he refuses to assist them they will plot for his death. The proverb encourages those on top to give those on the ground a ladder to climb up.

Like the Chinese maxim says: Give a child fish, you feed him for a day. Teach him how to fish and you would have fed not only him but many other dependents all their lives.

"The ants are never over burdened by any load," It is said. Ants especially the termite share their burden. There is division of labour in their Kingdom. This sharing of burden makes load lighter. Human beings should stop being self- centred and learn from the wisdom of the ants.

We know the case of Moses in the bible, when he was judging all Israel alone. He almost drove himself mad with loads of problems until his father-in law, Jethro advised him to delegate responsibilities to other people. That saved him from wearing himself out.

"When the wealthy oppress the poor, they are oppressing the maker" is a proverbial saying advising us that God created both the rich and the poor. Both parties are representatives of God and are serving different purposes. Any attempt to oppress the poor tantamount to oppressing God.

The Holy Scripture in James 5 advises thus: The very wealth you were counting on will eat away your flesh in hell. This treasure you have accumulated will stand as evidence against you on the Day of Judgment. For listen; hear the cries of the field workers whom you have cheated of their pay. The wages you held back cry out against you. The cries of the reapers have reached the ears of the Lord Almighty."

Our elders say "wealth is a visitor." It is an illustration that wealth does not stay at a place. Just as a visitor moves from one place to another, so also does wealth. But if you host it as you would host a good visitor, it may stay longer with you. It must be stressed that you need to nurture your wealth by investing and contributing to charity. Remember it is God that gives us power to make wealth.

In fact, one proverbial saying that may look extreme sees wealth as "the only visitor that deserves to be crippled". This is based on the belief that money does not stay in a place. It is a prostitute. In order to ensure that it stays with you when it comes is to ensure it is crippled or demobilized.

It must be emphasized that money deserves investing. We have to take proper care of it. Little wonder the saying that it is not good to neglect the goose that lays the golden egg. Money is important and deserves some modicum of care.

....

***When the wealthy oppress the poor,
they are oppressing the maker.***

....

'Success it is believed has many relations but failure is an orphan." When someone becomes wealthy or successful in life, people easily trace genealogy to the person. Even people who never knew him from Adam would want to trace affinity to him. But the reverse is the case when he is a failure.

Sometimes, some people make wealth yet it does not show in what they do. It is often said that nobody can hide if he becomes a millionaire. This is because the person's way of life, dressing and attitude must change.

He will surely start looking robust and if he goes to the bank, they are quick to attend to him.

But there are people you cannot fathom that they are rich. They are akin to the proverbial saying of "a man who has breast but prefers sucking stump." Such people, their relations are always taunted by others.

There was this wealthy man in my village. He was trained at the Massachusetts Institute of Technology (MIT) in the United States. He returned in the early 70s and got involved in many building contracts because he was an engineer. But nobody from the entire village benefited from his wealth. He never contributed to the development of the village.

And when anybody from our village goes to another to seek for help, they will shun the person. When we organize community development projects' launching wealthy people from neighbouring villages will not come because they believe we have a wealthy man they are all aspiring to be like. The agonizing aspect of it is that the man himself does not contribute to such development projects. It is even very difficult to see him in the village. All that shows such a wealthy man exists is the mansion he built at the express road that passes through our village and the structure is very conspicuous and painted all in white.

....

A man who has breast but
prefers sucking stump.

....

Chapter Twelve

UNITY

To say that unity is eluding mankind today is to state the obvious. The philosophy now is everyman to himself and God for all of us. No wonder there are conflicts upon conflicts everywhere. The truth about life is that without unity we cannot achieve anything as individuals.

Our elders say "when broom sticks are tied together, they sweep well." This saying supports the fact that there is much to be achieved when united. The Englishman said united we stand and divided we fall. Each of us has a peculiar gift God blessed him with. When we pull these gifts together, we will function effectively as a "common wealth" of nations.

This saying is strengthened by another which says; "when men urinate at a point at the same time, the urine foams" This is a positive effect of unity. It is the effort galvanized together that produced the foam (good result).

"Let the kite perch and let the eagle perch. Any of them that doesn't want the other to perch, should show it where to perch. "This proverb expresses peaceful co-existence. The world is too big and it can contain all of us. The resources of the world are too much to take care of us all. But it is the greedy and wicked who appropriate the resources of the world for their self-aggrandizement.

Most times, even what they don't need, they will appropriate it. Meanwhile, the person that needs that thing cannot lay hands on it. If only we can learn to be our brother's keeper as enjoined by the parable of the Good Samaritan in the bible, there won't be much strife on our planet.

This brings us to the problem of religious bigotry that is threatening to collapse the world now. Both Islam and Christianity were made by God. And God is love. If really, we are worshipping God as we claim, there shouldn't be any discrimination against Christians or Muslim. In fact, the worrying of it all is that the two religions have at their centre peace as the message. Why are we now selling violence. God will bring all to judgment.

More so, there is still racial discrimination in our society after so many years of ending apartheid. When has the skin pigment of somebody become the parameter for judging that person as a reasonable or successful person.

Tolerance should be our watch word. If we cannot tolerate ourselves, why are we then God's Homo sapiens?

"After all nobody can clap with one hand" says a proverb in Africa. Okay attempt clapping with one hand. How did you feel? Successful! Of course not.

This is a practical example that we all need each other. And we can only live in unity under peaceful co-existence. Africans are known for their communal life style. It is amazing now at the individualism life style that is gradually becoming the order of the day. This is wrong and will consume our race. It is better to learn from others. We are all witnesses to the problems created by individualism in the developed societies. A lot of them still envy our communal life style and would wish to be like us. So why can't we value what we have.

At least it is clear that governments of developed nations are spending fortune to take care of the elderly and little children in care homes. But we are our brother's keepers. This accounts for the reduced cases of depression in Africa as against the rising cases in the developed societies.

One of the reasons we're called human beings is because we were created to support one another. There is a saying that "when an animal's body starts itching, it scratches that part on a tree trunk. But when that of a man itches him, he asks his neighbour to assist him in scratching it." This makes us unique. When you need help you approach your neighbour, brother or friend.

But our individualism life style is gradually making bunkum of this good peaceful co-existence and this may make animals to be more united than us. At least it has been observed that elephants and gorillas care for each other. They even cry when one of them dies showing that man may not be the only creature with emotions. This should teach man many lessons.

Similarly, it is said that "when the right hand washes the left and the left washes the right both of them become clean." When we assist one another, we become liberated from our problems. There is strength in working together. At least we can borrow a leave from the ants that commune together and are never overburdened by any load. The maxim is akin to the other above that says nobody can clap with one hand.

Equally, it is said that "you cannot praise one side of a roof." The two sides of a roof add up to give a house its beauty. This proverb is used very well in settling dispute. It is not good to judge a case without hearing from the parties involved. It is when we had heard all that happened that we can give good judgment that will bring lasting peace.

The Yorubas of Western Nigeria have a saying that "if there is no crack in the wall, the lizard will not enter." Truly, if we don't divide ourselves, no outsider will. Most times we have problems, we created the opening for people to launch an attack on us.

This problem is common with newly married couple. They allow parents, friends, siblings and all sorts of outsiders to come in between them. A lot of them prefer settling their marital problems at the court of others instead of sitting down to find a lasting solution themselves. Those people we carry problems to even have more problems than we do but they decide to tackle them behind.

There is no perfect marriage. Any marriage without a problem does not exist. Couples should stop Washing their dirty linen in the public. Even the pastors we carry our matrimonial problems to have their own but they resolve them internally. It is said that "the man with protruding incisors have the boldest teeth." But there are people with bolder teeth whose lips covered them. Nobody talks about them as having big dentition.

> **If there is no crack in the wall,
> the lizard will not enter.**

And the saying that "it is the rat in the house that informed the bush rat that there is meat in the kitchen" is apt here. Most times we are the ones who invite outsiders into our lives and they wreck our unity and peace. "What is eating the vegetable is inside the vegetable" our people say. The earlier we stopped carrying our problems to third parties, the better for us.

Chapter Thirteen

COWARDICE

"**C**OWARDS DIE MANY TIMES BEFORE their death". This is a universal maxim known to many.

Bravery is highly rewarded in African societies. Any man that shows signs of weakness is derogatorily referred to as a woman. And men are usually trained in the art of bravery to defend their clan and villages. Part of what distinguishes a man from the woman is his ability to face challenges.

Many African societies initiate their youths (men) into many cults in order to make them strong enough to defend their communities. Age grade unions are encouraged. This is a way of building affinity amongst people of the same age grade and equally creating room for them to strengthen themselves in the art of bravery.

For those who show signs of cowardice amongst them, it is often said "you don't avoid battle because you are afraid you might be killed in it. "Many people sweep problems under the carpet instead of confronting them frontally. Problems are better solved and not dodged. When we dodge problems, we are just postponing the dooms day.

Apart from that, it tests your resilience and when you brave a situation you learn a lesson. It is better to be brave and fail than remain a coward without an experience. As has been observed over the years, the best form of defense is attack. If you retreat, your enemy will apprehend you and deal with you mercilessly. And as pointed out by the legendry Robert Nestor Marley (Bob Marley) the late reggae king, "He who fights and run-away lives to fight another day."

There are times we get overwhelmed by a task by just merely looking at it. We get seriously discouraged and start adducing all kinds of excuses. "The eyes are cowards" is a popular African proverb.

Truly, our sense of sight is controlled by the eyes. The eyes are responsible for sending impulses to the brain which are interpreted before sending the adrenalin for fright that controls our attitude of bravery or cowardice. Most times, the eyes interpret events in the negative. They see danger most times and it takes a brave heart to overcome such negative signals.

Although cowardice is seen as a vice and not a virtue in Africa, there are times when the coward is praised at the expense of the brave. Consequently, the maxim that "the coward protects both the life of the brave and his own."

Sometimes, the so-called brave man would want to approach a matter aggressively or with violence.

....

The eyes are cowards.

....

But the coward wouldn't cooperate with him. This may frustrate his effort and help prevent any harm that the action of the brave would have caused. Life's battle is not by power, nor by might but by the spirit of the Lord.

For example, there are times when an aggressor is ignored. He may punch you but you decide to run away from him. If you confront him, there might be a conflagration of the trouble and the consequences cannot be imagined.

Similarly, it is said that "sometimes it is better to be a coward. For we often stand in the compound of a coward to point at the ruins where a brave man used to live." The most important asset any man has is his life. Whenever he loses his life that is the end of him. People may taunt you into retaliating or urging you to be manly sometimes and fight back. Sometimes it is good to play the comic fool. Allow yourself to be used by enduring persecution or insult.

Whatever we do to preserve life is more than life. In an effort to restore the dignity of man and man is injured, it is a paradox. It pays sometimes to swallow insult. It is only the living that can praise God.

More so, there is a maxim that "the man who has not submitted to anything will soon submit to the burial mat". The brave man who is always ready for confrontation will sooner or later submit to a superior force and that will be his end. For one to think that he is invincible is to play God.

People who have this strong picture about themselves are those who believe in charms or magical Powers. They believe no man is strong enough to subdue them. But they forgot that when there is power encounter, the superior power will crush the smaller power into powder. Like the saying goes "one day monkey will go to the market and will never return again." Such negative power will one day fail such people when they needed it most. The bible says the hand of flesh shall fail.

In support of the argument that sometimes it is better to be a coward, it is said that "Laughter does not push anyone to the ground. It is man that purposely falls to the ground while laughing."

And it is not good to join issues with a fool for people will not notice the difference because the fool can bring you down to his level. He is a master of mire fight, where both the winner and loser are robbed with mud and nobody knows actually who the aggressor is.

Equally, it is said that "the toad likes water only when it is not hot." When the so-called brave man needs a fight, it is not when he sees somebody it is obvious that will defeat him. Our elders say that any man who doesn't know who is stronger than him isn't grown up yet. And when a man beats up the wife it's not a mark of bravery. After all, they are not equally matched and he cannot beat his chest that he has won a battle.

**The toad likes water only
when it is not hot.**

Chapter Fourteen

CRITICISM

ONE OF THE EASIEST THINGS to do in the world is to criticize. At least, at any point in time, the critic must see something to talk about either real or imagined. His criticism might not be supported by logic or common sense, but he may have followers who support whatever he says; These days there are a lot of arm chair critics. They just sit down at a place and feel they have better ideas of how everything should be done.

Our elders say "after observing a beautiful girl and there is nothing bad to say about her, the critic will say she is heady." This proverb goes to buttress the point that a critic must have something to say at any time whether backed up with facts or not. And being heady is not something to be discovered immediately. It takes some close observation and time to prove it. But the critic has said it and people around may swallow his opinion hook-line-and-sinker.

And we are in a world where people are excited in destroying others. They forgot the ancient saying that he who must destroy to live must have death as sentinel on his way.

However, this is not to conclude that all criticisms belong to the Pull Him Down (PHD) syndrome. There are objective and constructive criticisms that help some people to forsake their evil ways and become better citizens. This group of critics are not hatchet men who criticize because of what they can get. And they don't engage in non sequitur arguments just to score cheap points. They are interested in building and not destruction.

Chinweizu, one of Nigeria's best critics and prolific writers compared criticism to the manure which smells but makes plants grow. This kind of criticism falls into the objective group with an eye on development.

Proverbs being a mirror of the society tries to criticize people too. Its aim is to build, to refine and even to make the critic himself to pause and ponder. We must first of all remove the mote in our eyes in order to see clearly before removing those in the eyes of others.

For those who do not want criticism, it is better for them to hear this proverb which says. "If you don't want heat, you should not enter the kitchen." We all know that the kitchen is a place for cooking. And cooking emits heat. No matter how much anyone tries to make the kitchen cold, as long as food is being cooked there, it will get hot.

The proverb is simply a caveat for those who don't want to be criticized. Let them not get involved in anything that will attract public attention.

***If you don't want heat,
you should not enter the kitchen.***

Of course, we know that criticism is at the various levels of our lives. Even though we might escape from public criticism, that of the family, community or even groups we belong to as social animals, we cannot escape. In other words, criticism is inevitable in life.

Added to the above proverbs is another which says: "Anyone who knows his name is not good to be whistled with should never allow it to be used in whistling." Really, anyone who lacks the heart to take any criticism should try as much as possible to avoid anything that will attract it.

As pointed out earlier, not all criticisms are designed to destroy. When any one is criticized objectively and he complains he will be told this proverb: When you call a man by his name, it is not am offence." For instance, when somebody known to be a thief is called a rogue or the man with the gumming hand, he must not take offence for the critic has just told him what he is.

However, it is said that those who live in glass house should not throw stone. No body is infallible. The critic also is human and subject to mistakes. To tell the need for him to really be sure of his facts before criticizing, he must hear this proverb: "Until you walk in a man's shoes, don't laugh at the way he walks."

Many of us are quick to criticize others or run into hasty conclusions when we see people not doing what we expect them to do. Sometimes we don't have the patience to find out why they said or acted in the way and manner they did.

This problem is peculiar with journalists, members of the fourth estate of the realm. An average journalist is very critical when it comes to giving opinion on issues. Most times they don't have the patience to empathize with those they criticize. In fact, an average journalist has a better idea of how everything should be done. They are Jack of all trades and masters of all.

But the irony of it all is that if we start doing things or running governments according to editorials or opinions of the media, we will have a wacky world. Many journalists have been given positions of authority which they failed. But if it were others who messed up, the journalists will be the first to criticize.

The situation is like when you are watching people playing football, draught or scrabble games. When you are not playing, you seem to see many openings you can play and score high points. But when you come on board, it is all a different kettle of fish. Little wonder why the bible says we should remove the mote in our eyes before trying to remove those in other people's eyes.

More so, when we are pointing a finger at other people the other four fingers are pointing at us. This saying also goes to caution the critic to be careful and ensure that he is right in his criticism. This is because the measure we use in judging others will be the measure that will be used in judging us.

The bat says that "he knew he was ugly that is why he chose to fly in the night." When anyone knows he cannot take criticism let him not invite it. Let the person live a quiet, humble and obscure life.

But "a life not examined is not worth living" says a maxim. Nobody can write his testimonial. We all need others to examine us. And daily we go through all kinds of examinations in our homes, communities, offices, amongst peers, age grades etc. There can be no life without criticism just as there cannot be dream without sleep. And if anyone thinks because he will be criticized and refuses to do what he wants to do, he will never achieve anything.

Most achievers failed several times and where criticized severely. Such criticisms became the plank on which they became successful. Today their names are immortalized and the criticisms made against them are never remembered again. It is somebody who does not have a destination that is easily distracted by what others are saying.

Who knows how the world would have been without constructive criticism? Perhaps we would have been in Hobbesian era when might was right. For it is through criticism that the world has been able to do away with dictators and draconian leaderships. He who hates objective criticism hates quality life, freedom and social justice.

*A life not examined is
not worth living.*

Chapter Fifteen

PRIDE

PRIDE GOES BEFORE A FALL is a maxim known too well by many. Pride is a sin. I have not seen a society that condones pride. It was pride that made Lucifer lose his coveted position in heaven. It is an evil that pays no one. The result of pride is usually disastrous.

African society condemns pride roundly. Some proverbs have been coined to show disapproval to this obnoxious behaviour. "A man who never thought he could take an Ozo title usually ties the Ozo bangles on his arms and legs," It is said. It might be important to understand what the Ozo title means amongst the Igbos of South East Nigeria. It is one of the highest titles any man can be bestowed upon in the land. Most times, those given the title are wealthy because it costs a lot to carry out the ceremonies associated with it.

**_A man who never thought he could
take an Ozo title usually ties the
Ozo bangles on his arms and legs._**

Therefore when a man that never in his widest imagination thought he could take the Ozo titles is now bestowed with one, he becomes very proud and arrogant and puffs his shoulders like the puff Adder snake. He would want everybody around him to know he is one of the title holders in the town.

That reminds one of a certain don in my university days. If you call his name without putting the appendage professor, he will not answer you. If you send him a letter without addressing him as professor, he will return it back to the sender. If you eventually make the mistake of visiting his office and did not call him Prof, he will walk you out.

Meanwhile, his professorship was under dispute and the case was still in court. Yet he doesn't care. He forgot to understand that titles are loved by the inferiors and hated by the superiors.

Put in another way, "an empty vessel makes the most noise." Literally viewed, when you throw an empty drum on the ground, you cannot withstand the noise that will be associated with the action. But the reverse will be the case if the drum were to be filled with liquid.

This is the life of proud people. They want to be seen

and heard always. They talk on top of their voices anywhere you see them. They are always seeking for attention. And they are ready to do anything to get attention.

The situation is made worse when a proud man now achieves success in a particular thing. He would want people to worship him as God. This proverb gives credence to such situation. "Those whose palm kernels were cracked for them by benevolent spirits should never forget to be humble."*

Some of those who achieved success in life try to equate themselves with God. In some societies they play God and if you don't subscribe to their ideals you are eliminated. They refuse to learn from the case of Herod in the Holy Scripture who was eaten up by worms because he wanted to share God's glory with him. And as we know, the last thing God will do is to share his glory with anyone.

Our elders usually say that "when a man becomes successful where others have failed he thinks he is the only clever person." This is part of the problems of pride. It gives one a false impression of who he is. Success is meant to humble us and teach us lessons. But the reverse is the case. Man is supposed to know that in victory he should show humility and in defeat, gallantry.

When a man becomes successful where others have failed he thinks he is the only clever person.

PART 2

Chapter Sixteen

GENERAL PROVERBS

THERE ARE TIMES IN LIFE we take late action over an issue. The white man said: Make hay while the sun shines. It is better to arrest a bad situation before it gets out of control. In Africa, it is often said "it does no good to charm a snake after it has bitten." Of course, the predator has wreaked havoc already so what is the need of arresting it? In other words, "if the dog has bitten, driving it away is useless."

Another way of presenting this kind of proverb is: "We must bale this water now that it is only ankle-deep"*. Those whose homes have been flooded before will know the strength of this saying. If you don't bale water out of your house when it is ankle-deep, by the time it reaches the knee, you can hardly find where to rest yourself. The same thing applies to other problems of life. If you don't arrest a problem early enough it may become a big mountain which may be difficult to surmount.

....

We must bale this water now that it is only ankle-deep.

....

There is time for everything in life as pointed out in the book of Ecclesiastes. If you carry out a Programme or action at a wrong time you can hardly succeed. No wonder it is said that "if a child did not grow into maturity before searching for what killed the father, he runs the risk of being killed by the same thing."

It is advised that we should not be in a hurry sometimes to attend to some problems or issues. It is good to wait for the right time and atmosphere. If not, we will be endangered.

People give their children names to portray the fact that nobody knows tomorrow. It is said that "Nobody knows the womb that will bear a king." Truly, it is difficult to foretell from birth which child will grow up to become eminent member of the society. It is therefore not proper to condemn any one before he is given an opportunity to prove himself.

"When an evil becomes too much you confront it." Goliath was too much of an evil for the Israelites. God gave little David the courage to challenge him and he eventually defeated him. There are situations in life we've been avoiding but when the threat becomes too much, we can't but confront them.

This next proverb supports this situation. "There is an extent you respect a king after which you veil yourself and challenge him." We all know that Kings are not to be challenged. Their words are decrees. They have power to kill and make alive. When a King continuously comes up with unpopular laws or policies, one day he will be challenged.

This applies to many situations we find ourselves daily. There are situations we have been tolerating painfully because of many unexplainable factors. One day, we have to muster enough courage to challenge such situations. After all it is said that "a man can die but only once."

For those who would want to plunge into a task without thinking they should better listen to the next proverb. "You can't cross a log of wood with both legs at the same time. "We are expected to take precautions whenever we're dealing with any difficult task. It is said that "until the rotten tooth is pulled out from the mouth we must chew with caution." It does not pay to plunge into a problem. Only fools do that and the consequences are grave.

"When a pledge is made with empty hands days pass by in a jiffy. "The opposite of this proverb is what happens when you are in a problem. For instance, when you are sick or detained by the police, it appears as if 24 hours don't make a day any longer. Put differently, when you are writing an examination you never prepared for, it appears as if time flies.

As we go about our daily routine, it is difficult for us to tell all that we pass through. It is said that "the palm wine taper can never tell all he sees whilst up the raffia palm tree. In many African villages, houses are mainly huts sometimes without toilets and bathroom. And many activities go on oblivious of the sight of many. But the palm wine taper that climbs palm trees everyday catches an aerial and panoramic view of a village. Some of the things he sees, if he decides to reveal them, he will set the village ablaze.

"Ignorance is bliss" some people say.

However, when a man decides to manifest ignorance openly in place of knowledge, he will get this proverb: "When a man is not present when a corpse is buried, when asked to exhume the corpse he usually begins from the leg side of the grave."

Planning is very important in whatever we do in life. The man who fails to plan has planned to fail already. To stress the importance of planning, there is a saying that "A well planned battle does not claim even the crippled". We know that a lame man is physically immobile. And in a war, those who are immobile may not be able to escape. When a battle is planned, such people may be evacuated.

Let it suffice to say that when we have planned for things, we minimize risk, waste and save time and we produce better results. Things move generally smoothly when we plan in advance.

Being fastidious is one character some people manifest in our society. There is nothing you can do to satisfy such people even if you like kill yourself for them, it does not solve the problem. Thus, the saying that "there is nothing you can do for a lame man without him showing you his buttocks while leaving," is apt.

It is often said that "when an animal makes a swift move in the bush, a hunter also fires his gun swiftly." When a grown-up man behaves foolishly, he gets this proverb: "being tall does not mean one is grown up."

No matter the amount of money or success achieved by a child, he cannot claim to be higher than his parents or the elders of the society. After all it is said that "whosoever that owns a man owns whatever he has." If such child feels otherwise, he will be told that "no matter how tall an okra tree might be, it cannot be taller than the man who planted it."

The *okra* tree has slim stem the size of one inch rod. But it can grow up to ten feet tall. When the planter wants to harvest it, he does not need to climb it because the stem can't carry him. He does not need to climb anything or use any harvesting implement. All he simply does is to bend the stem of the plant and pluck the fruit.

We had this neighbour when I was growing up as a little boy in Port Harcourt, Rivers State Nigeria. The son was always coming last in any examination. In fact, children used to taunt him that he always comes first in the class from the rear. So, one day, after the boy had repeated primary three, three times, the father decided to see the headmaster to ascertain what was the problem and what solution was available. He woke up the morning he wanted to see the head-teacher and said to the wife, each time an arrow is fired from a bow it hits at a particular spot, does it mean that spot alone is meant for the arrow?" This is a proverb to show that you are tired of your stagnated position and desires a change by all means.

Our people say, "looking at a king's mouth, one would think he never sucked at his mother's breast."* Except a child whose mother died after delivery, every child sucks the mother's breast in order to survive. it has been proved that children who sucked their mothers' breast are more intelligent and are likely to resist many infant diseases. That is why many women are encouraged to breast feed their babies (baby friendly) instead of giving them cow milk.

The breast-feeding process has been identified also to engender close bond between mother and child. It has a humbling effect on the child which makes him grow up into a better member of the society.

There are times we achieve success and we become proud, walk shoulder high as if we are no more humans. The proverb above becomes apt for such situation. This is more important when the person rose from poverty or obscure background before attaining such height.

During the military intransigence in Nigeria, a general election held on June 12, 1993 said to be won by chief Moshood Abiola, a billionaire businessman and famous philanthropist was annulled. Mayhem was visited on the people as there were civil disturbances called out by the Civil Liberty Organizations (CLO), the Nigeria Labour Congress (NLC) and many other bodies. Many people were shot dead by security agents either overtly or covertly.

When Chief Abiola was asked what will happen to those who had died as a result of the struggle, the Egba Chief known for his free use of proverbs said "you cannot make Omelette without braking eggs." Some people can't but sacrifice their life in any struggle. Unfortunately, the Chief died in detention in an attempt to claim back his mandate.

Nevertheless, laughter does not connote happiness" it is often said. Many times, people try to wear a smiling face. Behind that face is an injured heart, a sick body or troubled mind. Many people hide under laughter to wreak havoc on others. Many describe the latter as toothy laughter. The person just shows you his front teeth and that is it. His smiling face or white teeth does not connect the heart.

Perhaps that is why the bible says that the heart of man is desperately wicked, who can fathom? Nobody! For as pointed out by William Shakespeare, "there is no art to find the mind's construction in the face."

"And laughter does not push anybody to the ground" Sometimes, some people laugh to the extent that they roll on the ground. It is definitely not the laughter that pushed them to the ground. They decided to fall.

In life, there are times you just ignore certain things because you want peace. Like some people say, you play the fool but you have a reason for doing that and it is what has made you 'stoop to conquer'.

Nobody likes threat. Threat builds all kinds of imagination in the mind of the person being threatened. Right now, the threat of terrorist attack by Al Qaeda on many nations is making governments of such nations lose sleep, preparing to foil or minimize the outcome of such violent attacks. That is why it is said that "it is only a tree you will tell that it will be cut down tomorrow and it will be there waiting." Anyone who remains passive while his territorial integrity is threatened cannot be a subject of tragedy.

Terrorist attacks are not just hatched overnight. They take several years before manifesting. the September 11, 2001 attacks on New York and Washington all in the United States of America, were planned several years before they struck. Some of the suicide attackers even trained in aviation schools in America. Nobody knew what they had in mind except themselves.

That is why it is said that "the thought that led to killing was not giving thought just one night" and that "the mind is cunning more than any other thing."

Sometimes people claim they want to help you to achieve certain things in life. You might discover that really you are the one making the effort and the people are taking the glory. In some instances, they may be assisting you with the right hand and at the same time using the left to ensure you never succeeded. It now turns out to the case of the proverbial man "carrying his friend on his back and the legs were touching the ground" It would have been better if he had allowed him to use his legs himself.

There are people who live with rich people but they can't afford two square meals. Some people have wealthy relations, yet life is so tough for them. And whenever they approach other people for help the people laugh because they believe their rich relations should be able to sort them out. The proverb that "it is not good for a man who has breast to be sucking stump" applies here.

Closely related to this saying is the proverb that a man living beside a river shouldn't wash his body with spittle" A person whose relation is in heaven is not supposed to go to hell it is said. It could be said to be ungodly or the highest manifestation of wickedness for somebody to be starving in the midst of plenty. It is only a fool that deserves this kind of treatment.

The book "Things fall apart" by Chinua Achebe painted a picture of Unoka, a loafer and big debtor who plots graph of his debts on the wall. When you visit him to settle his debts owed to you, he will show you the lines on the wall. If yours is a short line, sorry. He will tell you that "the sun will first shine on those standing before those sitting." Meaning he will pay his big debts first before the small ones. How ridiculous. Of course, it is a euphemism that he wasn't going to pay you.

Viewed broadly, the proverb tries to inform us that there are situations where some people have to benefit first before others. It might not be a healthy situation. But fairness is becoming elusive to many people.

Sequel to the above saying is the maxim that Eke

Atta market said it has not finished dealing with those standing how much less those sitting." We all know that in a crowd, those standing are more visible than others sitting. They have more advantage.

There are situations where those who have better chances have to be considered first before others. This is common in job interviews and entrance examinations for admission into schools and colleges or other things. Those with higher scores have to be considered first.

"The snake seen by one person is said to be python." This proverb can be said in another way. "The rod we use to measure the snake we saw alone is usually bigger." Exaggeration or hyperbole is employed many times when we want people to believe our story. Sometimes, we exaggerate to the extent that It becomes too obvious that we are lying.

There was a story of a Muslim 'Alhaji' who visited the holy land of Mecca for the first time. When he returned and was narrating his experiences, he told his friends that he saw at Mecca a fowl as tall as a three story house. His friends shouted Alhaji! Please reduce the size a bit. He said it was the size of two story house. The friends shouted again saying Alhaaaji, reduce it a little more. He said it was the size of a story building. They still urged him to reduce it. He became angry and shouted at his friends to go to Mecca and see the fowl themselves. What the Alhaji saw was an Ostrich. He was seeing such giant bird for the first time and had to exaggerate the size to sound impressive. So also most of us do when we try to impress others.

Somebody should be good for something. It is not proper for anybody to appear to be completely useless. There is nobody God did not endow with a gift in life. It is often said that "If a man doesn't know how to write, does it also means he hasn't got the ability to cancel?" While it is not good to compliment vices, but somebody should be known for something good. If you cannot do a great thing, you can do a small thing in a great way. All of us have gifts. We have to search for them.

This alludes to the saying that "If an in-law is not rich at least he should possess sweet tongue". With that, he will be able to defend himself where the wife's parents and relations are. It is not good to be like a defenseless building. A defenseless person receives insults always as can be deduced from this proverb below.

"There is an extent to which a son in-law may visit the father-in-law, one day he will be given a cutlass to go into the bush and get grass for goats" Of course, what this connotes is that the man's respect has whittled out.

"And when a blind man loses the 'udara' (berry fruit that grows in South Eastern, Nigeria) he found with his legs, who will give him another?" The chances of getting another is very slim. There are times we miss our opportunities of becoming great. Like people say, opportunity knocks but once. It is like the eclipse of the sun that happens once in a life time. This is not however to conclude that opportunity lurks around once. The only thing is that it does not lurk always and it is not easy to identify opportunities for they come most times masked as problems.

If an in-law is not rich at least he should possess sweet tongue.

The gathering of clouds shows that the atmosphere is heavy and it may rain. Whereas rainfall to the earth is regarded to be a blessing but it carries its own misery for some people. Our people say "when cloud gathers, the man with a leaking roof becomes restless."

Whenever a decision is to be taking on an issue, those it will negatively affect are always apprehensive. If there is any way they can stop the decision, they will. As rain does not tall on one root, no decision affects just one person. It could check a problem immediately and act as guide for the future.

An understanding of the maneuvering that goes on before a fowl is stolen will help to get the meaning of the saying that "whoever that has a child that steals fowls usually dies of heart attack." Those who steal fowls in the villages chase after them with sticks. Sometimes they set trap or cage for the fowls. In each of the method, the fowl struggles with the predator and it makes noise. Anyone who knows his child steals fowls, immediately he hears such noise around, the conclusion will be that the child has stolen or is about to steal another fowl and the person gets worried.

People who have children or wards who get into trouble always or bring odium to the family are often worried because they do not know what trouble the children will bring next.

A newspaper asked people to send in their opinion on the topic: "who is my friend?". The contribution that won the competition said "A friend is that person who comes in when every other person has deserted you". This contribution is almost same with the adage that says: 'When a corpse starts smelling, even the best of friends leave you."

Truly you can only know whom your friend is when you are in a bad situation or in need. You will discover that those people who wined and dined with you and you thought they loved you were just fair-weather people. The only person who can stand by you during the thick and thin of life is Jesus. He never tails and his love never ceases.

It is said that "when handshake passes the elbow it becomes another thing." When you indulge in excesses, Jesus is there to forgive you. Sometimes we knowingly or unknowingly indulge in excesses which bring problem to us. Equally, it is believed that "when a situation gets tough the end of the problem is in sight.

This saying is like a two-way traffic. The end may bring more misery but most times it brings good tidings. When you plant a seed, it will first of all die, get rotten before germinating. Sometimes, life's situations have to get bad before they get better. When you have reached the nadir of life you can't but bounce up.

The point where Jesus died and resurrected marked

the end of the spiritual power of death over mankind and the beginning of eternal life for us.

Most times we allow tough times to consume us.

We organize pity party for ourselves. Tough times are there to teach us some lessons. They are there to bring out that ugly part of us that is hidden so that we can become better people. There is no promotion without a test. Only those who endure till the end will win the crown. Anyone who chickens out on the way is not meant for the crown.

It was pointed out earlier in this book that proverb could be vulgar. In the vulgarity, what we are interested in is the good message it impacts on man. It is like manure. Though it smells but it also makes plants to grow.

A critical observation of the way the male genital reacts when it's about to have sex will assist us to understand the proverb that says "when the penis wants sex, it begins to act as if it will pull down a roof". We know how stiff the penis could be when it wants sex. Sometimes it nods like the redneck lizard chasing after its female partner. As soon as it has performed its function, it gets weak and reduces drastically in size and strength.

The same thing applies to some situations in life. There are some people who show great strength at first over some situations in life. Even in the religious circle, some people get over zealous and fanatical. But any slightest obstacle, they give up and back-slide, like the penis.

Similarly, it is said that "when you abuse sex you Will know that the female anatomy has teeth. My cousin used to have a driver that could be addressed as a sex maniac. Any night he slept alone, the next morning he will be very uncomfortable and unease. During that period, he had all kinds of sores on his genital.

***When the penis wants sex it behaves
as if it will pull down a house.***

This proverb is a lesson to those who engage in excesses like drug abuse, Kleptomania and even nymphomania. Too much of everything is bad. Life's best philosophy is moderation.

Chapter Seventeen

DENTIFYING A PROBLEM IS THE beginning of solving it. Sometimes, good things come as problems. It takes understanding, experience and patience to identify this kind of 'problem' "If you get hold of the head of a snake, the rest of it is mere rope" is a proverb that attests to the saying above. When you deal with a problem head-on, it gets solved. Some people prefer dealing with problems with kid gloves. Problems don't understand gentle language. You have to confront problems frontally. Problems are better solved and not evaded. Remember the saying that he who fights and runaway lives to fight another day. And that since the time of John the Baptist, the Kingdom of God suffers violence and the violent take it by force.

And no matter how good you wash a pig, it must return to the mud. "This proverb could be said in another way thus "A dog must return to its vomit. Have you not seen some people who returned to crime despite all the efforts made to keep them of it? Some people say it is poverty or deprivation that causes crime. Yet there are people whose parents are rich and give them all they need. But they still go back to stealing other people's properties. Sometimes what they steal is worthless and unimaginable.

If you get hold of the head of a snake, the rest of it is mere rope.

This proverb points out such attitudes people always go back to. They are like acceptable standard of living for such people. To some of the people indulging in this kind of behaviour, they seem not to see what they do as evil. Their case is like that of a mad man who said "he knows what he is doing but does not know what is happening to him." Such people deserve the sympathy and empathy of the public to come out of the problem. They must not be isolated.

The above proverb is supported by the saying that "No matter the cure given to a mad man, he must murmur" Murmuring is a major character of any mad person even after being cured. It is the scar of madness. This saying points out that there are people, no matter what you do for them, they will never be grateful or they will never change from their evil way. After all, it is said that "the leopard will never lose its spots.

Our elders said "whatever the leopard sired must not be different from the leopard". It is what a man has that he bequeaths to the offspring. It is a natural thing. It is genetic. When a child does not have any of the genetic traits of the parents, it becomes doubtful! if they are the biological parents of such child.

In the spiritual realm, it is called familial spirit. It is a way, a particular family or group that are biologically related either closely or remotely behave. When somebody known to come from a particular group behaves in that way and manner they are known, it is no more strange. If the person behaves contrary, then it will raise eyebrow. it is like the journalistic saying that "When a dog bites a man is no news" because dog is expected to bite man. When man bites a dog, it is an abnormality and hot news.

Many people want to be like some other persons. We all want to be celebrities. "As a man is so also is his problem" says a proverb. There was this story of a poor man who approached a certain rich man to help him become rich. When the rich man told him what he must do to become rich, the poor man begged the rich man to allow him remain in his poor state.

After all, "there is beauty in ugliness." And it is said that "there is something good in being mad only know to mad people". No body is completely useless and no situation is completely bad. Failure is not bad just as death is not the end of all things.

Without the ugly, you will not know the beautiful. Without failure, you wouldn't appreciate success. And not everybody can be rich, just as not all will be poor. Whatever position one finds himself, there is an important role he is playing. There is a void he is filling; that is contributing to the general wellbeing of the society. If everybody becomes conformist, the world will be a boring place.

Obviously, "you can only tell a blind man there is no oil in the soup and not pepper or salt". A blind man has his sense of taste what he lacks is the sense of sight. It will be wrong or foolery for anyone to tell him there is no salt or pepper because it is too obvius. Some things are too obvious for people to know themselves.

Similarly, "you can foretell the taste of a man's faeces by the smell of the fart." There are events which take place and you can easily predict the next thing that will follow. It is often said that "you have to see the face of a woman that gave birth to a baby before asking her to show you her baby." When a woman has a safe delivery, it is all too obvious. When the baby is delivered dead or with some complications it will manifest in the mother's mien.

Some people behave as if they have the monopoly of violence or unleashing terror on others. For such people, they need to see their kind for them to stop such obnoxious behaviour. "A mad dog has not seen a mad fox" it is said. When there is equal strength, peaceful resolution is in the offing. Why there are so many injustices today in the world is because of inequalities in strength that exist between people, communities, and states.

Nepotism has assumed a big position in our society. People favour their relations, friends, or neighbour at the expense of others. Even the principle of equality which many countries ascribe to themselves does not hold water as many people still go the extra mile to favour their acquaintances and friends triggering the saying that "you cannot over feed your son because you believe he is the incarnate of your dead father."

Bad neighbourhood is a problem many communities are faced with. If some people know that their neighbour will behave badly may be they wouldn't have agreed to live close to them. A fable has it that the anus told the female anatomy that "if he knew she will be receiving so many visitors, he wouldn't have accepted that they become neighbours"

The next proverb however seems to provide an answer to the former. It is said that "if you want to have friends, you should be friendly yourself". Many times, we complain about other people not being friendly or favourably disposed to us when we have not made any effort to present a friendly front to them. There is no person shown genuine love that does not reciprocate it.

Practice this; if you have a neighbour or a colleague who does not talk to you or who feels with-drawn, make it a point of duty to greet the person, smile at him, enquire about his welfare. If he rebuffs you the first two days, the third day, he must respond favourably to you. What many people do is to conclude at first sight that their neighbour is snobbish or egotic without really sounding him out. One person definitely has to initiate the stimulus for a relationship to be developed and sustained.

Equally, it is said that "you cannot predict how a market day will be by simply concluding with the early happenings on the day of the market." As pointed out above, it will be erroneous to conclude that your neighbour is snobbish or proud by merely looking at him or through the casual response he gave to you on the first day you met.

This perhaps informed the saying that leave whatever is written on a vehicle and board the vehicle". the fact that the vehicle bears on its body the Inscription "I shall return" does not mean it cannot run into a tree or plunge into the river the next moment. We must not be discouraged by the things we see. All we see are ephemeral but the things we do not see are eternal.

When we are carried away or discouraged by what we see, it shows we don't have faith. And without faith it is impossible to please God, for faith is the substance of what is not seen but believed. It is that hoped for. It is like the muscle that develops and gets stronger with usage. So, don't forget to exercise your faith if you want good things to come your way.

Our elders say "when darkness comes it appears as if the day will never break". Initially, exercise of faith may not produce quick result and it may be easy to conclude that the step taken was on the wrong path and we get weary. But there is always light at the other end of the tunnel for those who persevere.

Sometimes some people wilfully seek for other people's problem. People who do this can learn from this proverb which advisably said "the rat should not wilfully rip open the fetish doctor's goatskin bag and the fetish doctor should not wilfully roast the rat's mouth in the fire". Live and let live is the best philosophy of peaceful co-existence.

Nothing is worth dying for in life. "There is nothing the eye will see and cry out blood" is a saying to stress the above statement. As stated by Aristotle, one of the classical philosophers, "You cannot succeed in saying a new thing." Everything has been said in one way or the other. All we do is to copy, paraphrase or rephrase. Even as pointed out by Solomon in Ecclesiastes, there is nothing new under the sun. Therefore, let no one kill himself over anything. It is said that "the millipede that was crushed did not complain rather the man that crushed it with his leg is complaining bitterly that it has soiled him." Sometimes, your adversaries or attackers are quick to complain instead of you that was injured or hurt. This is a big irony of life.

In some cases, this could portray one as being very desperate. And as stressed in this proverb, "A man with a running stomach doesn't care about a sacred bush dedicated to a god. When a man is desperate, he does not see, feel or sense danger. "He that is down needs fear no fall a hymn says.

When people lack the ability to do something, they

give impossible conditions before they can carry out the task. The saying that "A native doctor that lacks the ability to heal a patient will ask the relations of the sick to bring the eye of an ant as an ingredient for producing a portion for healing, attests to that.

Consequently, it is said that "people's misfortune is the native doctor's fortune." Whenever there is a problem there are people who are bound to reap from it. Have we bothered to find out from arms dealers why they supply weapons to a rebel group fighting a government? Some people are experts in crisis management. Even in the worst economies, some people are well off.

This reminds me of the story of a casket seller. In a certain village it was said that most businessmen were complaining of poor sales and the casket dealer also joined them. Of course, what he wants is for people to die. And whose person will die?

"The man who likes to eat funeral meat, why does he recuperate from illness?" There are people who derive joy at the sufferings of others. They would want you to lose your own asset but they wouldn't want theirs to go. Upon that they will want to share from your asset. If you refuse to give them, there is trouble.

My grandfather used to say while alive that "a man with good genital does not appreciate what the others suffering from the elephantiasis of the scrotum are passing through." Many people who find themselves in a better condition don't really appreciate what others who are not so endowed are experiencing. It would have been better for situations in life to rotate round so that those who are well disposed can experience bad side of life and compare note. This will make many people to thank God for his kind mercies on them.

When my late mother was ill, I visited her in the hospital where I saw people who were feeding through tube and some others with their legs hanged. I was humbled. Ever since that visit, every morning, I kneel down to thank God for his kind mercies.

Have you seen a snake swallowing another? I have seen. It is not a good sight. It is said that "when a snake swallows another, the tail of the swallowed snake protrudes out." Apart from this being abominable, the snake that swallowed the other can never enjoy peace until what it ingested dies, becomes rotten and gets digested.

You can then imagine when a man kills his fellow man or relation how it will look like. The saying is applied most times when somebody that shares the same faith with you now wants to harm or defraud you. Where is the esprit de corps or spirit of camaraderie?

"When a man kills somebody, he will be responsible for the burial, has he achieved anything?"

"Rain cannot fall without the ground knowing it. "Rainfall must touch the earth, that is how nature made it. If it doesn't touch the ground, it is no more rain. In other words, there is nothing hidden under the sun. Many people commit atrocities in the dark or in their closet and conclude that nobody saw them. If no eye saw them, the walls, bushes, rivers have eyes and ears. They will testify against such persons one day.

Apart from that, God created the universe and His eyes are moving to and from the earth. He sees all our evil deeds in the dark. For light shines into darkness and darkness cannot overpower it. No matter where you are, you are under the watchful eyes of God. His eyes are more than close circuit television (CCTV) which many are afraid of yet they are not afraid of God Himself.

If faced with the choice of relating with people, it is easier to relate with close relations and siblings before others. It is just natural. There isn't much anyone can do about that. The proverb that "It is after tracing your relationship from your mother's lineage then can you start thinking of that of your paternal line", becomes appropriate here.

It is through this that you will be able to find out the veracity of the saying that "whoever is nearer to a mouth knows how it smells." The nearer, the warmer people say. Many people stay afar to appreciate or condemn things. It is when we draw nearer to such things that we will be able to really know how they are. Then, we can make value judgment. When we see things from afar, the likelihood is that we may misperceive them. And our misperception may lead to misconception which may likely mislead us.

And when we are nearer to people it is better for us to comport ourselves. There is no need being overzealous. If not we might be seen like "the man invited to a dinner who ate more than his host". This is because "a stranger is not expected to weep more than the bereaved in a funeral". If not, the people around may misinterpret the communication. We should not carry other people's problems on our head. It is important to realize that "the inquisitive monkey gets the bullet."

My grandfather also told me that "if I am faced with the decision to choose between a road and a cow, I should choose the road. "I asked him why? He said, when you choose a cow, you can slaughter the cow, eat it up or sell it and that is the end. But when you choose the road, you will continue to make use of it. Let it suffice that the old man was advising me on the importance of building bridges of relationship. He explained that any man that has relations or friends does not lack anything. The people the person met along the road will always come to his aid if he developed good relationship with them. Whereas the reverse is the case with the cow. The cow connotes a one- off- thing.

Beyond this, he advised that I should be nice to people I meet on my way as I climb the ladder of life for, I will still meet them on my way back. The graph of life is like that of a linear equation graph. When a child is born, he grows up into adulthood, later in life he grows into old age when he starts behaving like a little child again.

It is the good relationship built in this journey of life from childhood to old age that will sustain you when frail and perhaps immobile, he stressed.

Age, however is not like a linear graph. As tall as a man is, does not determine his age. These days, teenagers grow as tall as seven feet while the elders grow shorter. Nobody can tell the value of anything by just sheer size.

That will be a naive way of judgment. It is like judging anything by merely looking at the appearance. This is one of the worst ways of passing judgment. Appearance is not reality. And all that glitter is not gold.

Isaac Newton one of the greatest physicists the world ever produced propounded the law of gravity which stipulates that whatever goes up must come down. True as this may be, it has been observed in Africa that "whatever goes up does not come down except people's age."

In Africa, it is very common to see the cost of living going up without coming down. It is easy to see inflation perpetually hanging high without any plan to fall. Whilst this is happening, many find it difficult to meet with their plans in life. Many university graduates stay for five years and above before securing employment which is not commensurate with their qualification. The problem is even more with the female folks who are facing pressure from many angles which includes getting married and raising children since their life is time bound.

Consequently, because of this inability to meet up these demands of life, people reduce their age always. Many people don't ever present their birth certificate as is the case in the developed society.

Rather, they present age declaration (sworn court affidavit). As years pass by, many people swear more affidavit of age declaration. It is common to see a man having more than two age declarations.

Even those who are already employed, swear

affidavit to reduce their age so that they will not be retired. They forgot that if they don't leave the service their productivity will reduce and the entire system will suffer. Also, they forgot that their children who are out of school cannot be employed.

I have a friend who chucked out a whooping seven years out of his age. But there is no cheating nature. Our elders say "when suffering visits a man and the man tells him there is no seat for him, he tells the man not to bother because he brought his own stool." So, there is no running away from old age no matter how many age declarations we swear to.

It must be remembered that it is said that "when you impregnate a woman standing, she delivers a mad child". When things are done hurriedly, most times the result is not good. It is important that we approach every task with all the carefulness and attention it demands before we bungle it because of hurriedness.

One of Newton's laws of motion states that "action and reaction are equal and opposite". This law is a natural law. It is the same with the law of sowing and reaping or karmic reaction. No matter our belief, the law applies to us. It is like a man's buttocks which follows him behind no matter how fast he pretends to run. No wonder it is said that "when you give a little child a bad push, a bad curse flows from his mouth."

It is the measure we give that we will receive in return. A little boy is supposed to respect an elder. But when an elder now throws caution away and gives him a bad push, of course the child will return fire for fire.

Meanwhile, "when you take a decision behind a strongman, you will likely change the decision." Every society has its own strongman. Every group has a strongman. In those days, he used to be somebody physically endowed who had brought home many human heads from inter-tribal wars. These days in Africa, the strongman could be a money bag, witch doctor, politician, top civil servant etc. In fact, any one that calls the shots at any time is the strong man. And because he wields some influence and power, if not consulted in any decision making, he may upturn the whole decision.

After the annulled June, 1993, presidential election in Nigeria that caused a lot of political quagmires, Chief Francis Arthur Nzeribe, a notable multi-millionaire and politician from the South East part of the country was accused of playing a prominent role in truncating the election believed to have been won by Chief Moshood Kashimawo Abiola, a businessman and billionaire from the South West.

It was believed that Chief Abiola now late, had à secret meeting with some top members of their party the Social Democratic Party (SDP) now defunct, where it was decided that the party could win the presidential election without the support of the South East, which has the third biggest ethnic group in the country.

Chief Nzeribe, a top notcher of the party was not invited to the meeting. And he discovered that out of the top six political positions in the country, none was zoned to the South East where he comes from. He vowed secretly to work against the success of that election and the outcome was the annulment of the result.

After the annulment, Chief Abiola realized that he made a mistake by neglecting Chief Nzeribe and his ethnic group. He had to pay the latter a visit at his country home to appeal for cooperation towards revalidating his mandate. But the milk had been spilt.

Chief Nzeribe later said in a press statement in the newspapers that he knows he cannot be the president of Nigeria. He cannot even be the vice president. But whoever that wants to rule him must consult him or he will spoil business for the person.

"Whatever tune you play in the compound of a great man there is always someone to dance to it" is a proverb which portrays the strength and versatility of a great man. Whatever anybody wants in such a stead whether good or bad, he must get it. The great man's stead is an amalgam of the good, the bad and the ugly. It is good for outsiders going in there to thread with caution.

Sometimes people take rash decisions by following unpopular courses. It is like a politician who decides to join an unpopular party in his constituency, if he decides to seek for support, he may be told that "it is not good to leave where people are taking ozo title to where sacrifices are made to shrines. "For when a fowl fouls the air the ground pursues it."

When I was in the University, there was this course mate of mine that was always complaining. When it shines, she will complain. When it rains it is another problem. She was too fastidious that nobody took her complaints seriously anymore. Thus, alluding to the saying that "a child that cries always does not make it easy for people to know when he is thoroughly beaten." Truly when the lady had genuine complaint, the head of department never took her seriously. She had to repeat a year.

It is however said that "when a crying child continuously points at a place, it is either the father is there or the mother." When an issue is stressed continuously it is important that serious attention is paid to it because it could be that something that affects somebody's life or the fabric of the society. Another way of stressing this is: "When an old woman stops very often in her gyration to point repeatedly at a particular direction, we can be sure that somewhere there something happened long ago which affected the foundation of her life."

In our society today, it is becoming increasingly difficult to help people with genuine needs. This is due to there are many people who are faking to have one problem or the other. "The appearance of mechanics makes it difficult for us to know who is a mad man."

In Africa, most motor mechanics wear rags or discarded clothes instead of work overall. Except you know them or deal with them you may find it difficult differentiating any of them from the lunatics. This observation gave birth to the above saying.

An adage has it that "when the lion becomes lame, even an antelope can confront it" When a brave man becomes incapacitated, people who under normal circumstances cannot approach him will now have the opportunity of even speaking rudely to him.

> **A child that cries always does not make it easy for people to know when he is thoroughly beaten.**

In fact a similar adage says "when a big tree falls to the ground, even the women can climb it" Big trees like lroko are not easy to be climbed by the men how much less the women. It is only very few men trained in the art of tree climbing that can climb such big trees.

But when such tree falls to the ground, even the women can climb the trunk and branches. Sometimes they use the branches as fire wood. This tells us what people can do to a great man who has fallen from grace to grass.

Added to this, it is said "nobody climbs an Iroko tree twice." There are a lot of things involved before people climb such trees. Sacrifices are made to gods because it is believed some of the trees are the abodes of the gods. Apart from that they are big and demand some expertise before they can be climbed.

Equally, there are some tasks one need not embark on twice. They are so daunting or risky that immediately you succeed in the first attempt, you make proper use of the opportunity and give it up.

Many people in Africa engaged in hard and risky businesses like hard drug peddling and politics use this proverb very often. This philosophy may have contributed immensely to the under development of many African societies.

A lot of people in position of trust see it as a once in a life time opportunity. Because of this, they amass as much wealth as they can at the expense of the public they are supposed to be representing. This is one of the reasons why corruption is very rampant in Africa and budgetary allocations are never utilized for what they were meant for. Even when you don't have such spirit to embezzle, you will be reminded of the proverb above.

But the proverb is not a truism. There are many people who have been appointed to public positions two or more times. Chief Olusegun Obasanjo, Civilian President of Nigeria from 1999 to 2007, was once the country's military head of states. Flight Lieutenant Jerry Rawlings now late, was a military head of state of Ghana before serving as civilian president for two terms. People should stop this wicked saying that puts others under pressure to embezzle public funds.

Chapter Eighteen

N AFRICA, "SOMETIMES WHEN WE give a gift to a child, we may ask the child to give us a little from what was given to him just to know his reaction, not because we really want to eat." Equally, in life, there are certain actions we take, not that we mean it, but rather we want to test public opinion.

In the same vein, "when you give a child a big gift, he enquires from you who he is to share it with. "Surprise they say is a game. Sometimes it is good to surprise people. You confuse them and make them change their impressions about you. An element of surprise is always good for life. It gives fresh insight to life.

Of course, a clear conscience fears no accusation just as "a man not carrying any burden is not over burdened by any yoke." No matter how much people try to paint you black or cause trouble for you, you will surely overcome. Truth, they say is like a football on top of water. No matter how much effort made to push it down the water, it must surely come to the top. Truth is as stiff and straight as a man's raised genital "our elders said.

> ***When you give a child a big
> gift, he enquires from you
> who he is to share it with...***

At times we try to get involved in things we do not have the expertise or knowledge. To some people anything goes. But they forgot the saying that "a dance step learned in old age is usually stiff". At such age people are no more malleable. That is why some employers find it difficult employing people of certain age group. There is no new trick you can teach an old monkey.

"It is not compulsory that a corpse must be buried in an already dug grave" our elders say. There are times we behave as if our lives depended on a certain thing. Nothing is compulsory. Like a friend used to say, everything is optionally compulsory". It is compulsory but optionally. It depends on the individual concerned. Therefore, when somebody tells you that if certain things are not done there will be no peace or respite, it is better to let the person know the above proverb.

There is this story in Chinua Achebe's "Things

fall Apart", where Okonkwo, the tragic protagonist suffered several misfortunes. When they consulted the oracle, they were told that the late father wanted him to sacrifice a goat for him. He replied and said: "Ask my father if when he was alive, he had a fowl?" He never offered any sacrifice to the late father and that may not have been responsible for his problem. As pointed out earlier, "when a man says yes, his personal God (chi) says yes." It is a matter of faith.

After all, "the size of a man's eyes does not determine how far he sees things." Good sight is not dependent on size of a man's eyes. The success of a thing is not dependent on the size. We all know that the owl has big eye balls. But it doesn't see in the day. The same thing applies to bats.

The latter is a reminder. The bat says "he knows he is ugly that is why he chose to fly in the night" Some people know their weakness and have equally put in place survival strategies to overcome it. There are others who allow their weakness to eat them up. Life is a struggle. In a warfare you don't fold your hands. You attack if not your enemy will take you hostage.

Nothing goes for nothing in life. It is said that there is no free lunch anywhere in the world. The people giving you a supposedly free lunch are investing in you. If not for any other thing, they expect your loyalty. When a man gets your loyalty what else is he asking for?

An adage says that "he who eats the scrotum of a ram is indebted to elephantiasis of the scrotum." When a man does a favour to you, you definitely owe him. This proverb is akin to the one immediately above. There are people who keep accepting favours from people with the plan not to reciprocate or pay back. No matter how much the person pretends or tries to forget that some favours were meted out to him, the conscience will not forget. Othman Dan Fodio, the leader of Islamic Jihad in Nigeria said "Conscience is like an open wound which only truth can heal". In fact, you cannot see a newly born baby's first set of teeth with an empty hand. Our culture demands that you buy a fowl in the child's honour or give some money to the mother for the baby's sake.

> ### *Conscience is like an open wound which only truth can heal.*

No matter how long anyone cries, his tears will not blind his eyes" says an Igbo adage. They are therapeutic. When we cry, we purge ourselves of excess emotion. Tears serve cathartic purpose. There are certain things we feel are bad when they happen to us but they are blessings in disguise.

"It is prettily difficult to tell if a tortoise is in its youth or it's an adult." Only experts or a close look at a tortoise can reveal its real age. This is a lesson to man. There are matured people who have not been able to do anything to properly position themselves. Any time you see them, they are still behaving and acting like little children. They can't stand up and be counted whenever the need arises.

There are times, some people engage others in mud fight. They try to pull other people to their level and it takes only careful observation by outsiders to really know who is at fault. You know in mud fight, everybody is rubbed with mud. But the truth is that "he who threw another down in a fight and held him down on the ground is also holding himself." It is only when he leaves the person on the ground can he stand up himself.

It is only when our adversaries decide that we can have peace, that they can have peace too. "The child that says the mother will not sleep, how can he sleep?" As Shakespeare pointed out in the tragic drama, "Macbeth", Macbeth has murdered sleep, Macbeth shall sleep no more, Duncan shall sleep no more."

In another development, it is said that "only a fool would stand afar to kick at another person." You need to draw nearer before you can kick the person. If you want to know what the sophists are doing,you have to join them and study sophism. The nearer, the warmer it is said.

It is like saying you are a Christian and you still work in darkness. God is light and those who worship him are children of light. "If we draw nearer to God, he draws nearer to us. Let us not be like the barber who keeps moving round his client while the client is just at a place.

When you did not offend somebody, there is nothing

he can do to harm you that will succeed. The bible says that surely, they shall gather but because they have not gathered in the name of the Lord, their gathering is in vain. Also, Isaiah 54 v 17 says. No weapon fashioned against me shall prosper and every tongue that shall rise up against me in judgment I should condemn for such is the heritage of the servants of the Lord and our righteousness is of the Lord.

"The fly that perches on a mould of dung may strut around as it likes, it cannot move the mould." No matter what our enemies do, they can't succeed in harming or killing us except God permits them.

And "it is from a man's own stock of sense that he gives out to his son." It is what a man has that he can give out. It is genetic and spiritual. When a man starts giving what he does not have, it is either he has started stealing or he is deceiving people. This is strengthened by the adage that "the offspring of a hawk cannot fail to devour ducks."

If a man is evil, he is not expected to impart into the children good things. A Mango tree must bear mango fruit. If it bears berry, definitely something is wrong. "A woman cannot place more than the length of her leg on her husband", it is said.

Many people are made to believe that there is an El Dorado somewhere they can go and their problems will be over. This thought is greatly responsible for the increase in migration to Western Europe and the United States. Given that these areas have better economy, "there is no city without its own fair share of lunatics."

No city is self-sufficient. There are problems peculiar to every city. It takes people in that city to know the problem.

For instance, most cities in Western Europe and America are under siege of insecurity, terrorist attack, obesity, suicide, depression, divorce and all kinds of diseases western science cannot name. But somebody hearing about these places in Africa will take an oath that he will never die until he had migrated to them.

The sickness that will kill a man starts with appetite". Similarly, "the sickness that kills a man will be buried with the man." Whatever negative trait that we refuse to give up, will accompany us to the grave. As John Maxwell pointed out "Our destiny is determined, not by what we possess but what possesses us."

A man's destiny can be delayed but not terminated. Sometimes we try to use our physical effort in trying to achieve things. If what we are struggling for does not belong to us, no amount of effort can make us achieve it. Life successes are not by power nor by might but by the grace of God. "If a man holding a little child's property raises his hands up, when his hands start aching, he will surely bring them down."

When people wilfully deprive you of your right, don't give up. Be steadfast in doing good sooner than later, they will be tired and hand over to you that which rightly belong to you. It is just a matter of time.

Any government that robs Peter to pay Paul must only count on Paul for support. Our society is full of one kind of discrimination or the other. If you are not segregated against because of the pigment of your skin, it may be of your tribe, height etc. The irony of it is that the same people who discriminate against you still want you to be loyal to them. This is not easy to achieve. "When you treat people equally, you eliminate envy and strife."

Nobody likes public disgrace. It is very shameful. It is even more shameful when the person involved is wealthy and known. "It is better to kill a wealthy man than to openly disgrace him," A question may be asked: Is there any smoke without fire? A wealthy man may not just be disgraced for nothing. He may have caused the public odium.

A contrary proverb says: "if you expose an illness, it gets cured." There are many obnoxious behaviour people have. Some of them are exhibited in the private. For instance, a man that masturbates, it will take serious surveillance and spying to discover this. When it is found out, you don't hide it. Expose it. This is the only way such problem can let the person it is holding bound, free.

"A fowl does not forget anyone that pulled off the tail feather during the rainy season." People don't usually forget people who came to their aid in time of need. The memory of such good deed is kept alive if it happened at a particular time that serves as a reminder to the beneficiary.

King Solomon in Ecclesiastes pointed out that there is time for everything under the sun. Truly time is very important in our life here on earth. It is the determinant of many things. It is one commodity both the poor and rich have equally. It is said that "Any tree that reaches its time to bear fruit will bear some". At any stage in life, the society expects people to do that which that stage approves. When somebody gets into a particular stage and refuses to act in line with the expectations of that stage, people want to know why. The person may be said to be fixated in the stage he was in already.

Although this has a way of helping people to aspire to achieve, it also puts enormous pressure on them. The tendency is that some people may have to employ some obnoxious means by circumventing the 'burden' society places on their shoulders. And like one philosopher pointed out, "man's goal is the cause of crime."

"If the first son in a family does not behave like a lunatic, the father will not marry a wife for him. "Sometimes in our society, people are taken for a ride. Except such people rise up and challenge whatever obstacle the family or society places on their way, they will never achieve what they are supposed to achieve.

It is a type of forceful advancement. There are situations you must confront in your life or they will keep you perpetually pinned to the ground. We saw how Jacob wrestled with an angel of the Lord in the bible. He insisted that the angel must bless him if not he will not let him go. Truly, he was blessed and his name was changed from Jacob, the supplanter to Israel. Through this, Abraham's promise by God that he will be the father of multitude was realized.

Rendering help to one another is very important

for life to progress. Nobody can clap with one hand. But there are times when people give us help and we expect more helps. They may likely get this response: "If I marry for you, will you expect me to lay a mat for you to sleep with your wife?" Definitely, we have to help ourselves also. It is said that when a man falls into a pit and raises his hands for help he will be helped but when the person decides to fold his hands and resign to fate or assume that people will know he is there, he will remain there.

"When you shoot a lizard according to the way and manner it posed on the wall, your gun powder will be exhausted." There are situations in life we need not approach with the same vigour they appear. Some of such situations are purposely put on our ways to distract or overwhelm. They need to be approached with caution. "It is with utmost care that we can lick hot pepper soup without harming ourselves."

But the lizard that fell down from a huge iroko tree looked left and right, not seeing anyone applauding it, nodded the head and said "if no one deems it fit to praise me, I will praise myself." There are times you achieve a feat and nobody congratulates you on your effort. You don't allow that to weaken you. Cheer up.

After all, "all the lizards lying down nobody knows which one is suffering from stomach ache." We see different kinds of people every day going about their business, we don't really know what difficulty each of them is passing through except any of them tells us. That is why it is not good for anyone to want to be like another person. God created each of us uniquely. If the person we want to be like tells us the problem he is in, we will thank God for his mercies.

Blame shifting is a common thing in life. When we refuse to do the right things and the consequences come, we blame our foundation, stars or even God. I have a friend who is always blaming God for failing to give him a good job. The man wants a high-flying job but he is not even educated. He cannot even express himself well in spoken English. This buttresses the saying that "when a harlot starts ageing, she starts telling people she is being disturbed by mermaid spirit."

"A fowl with high tendency for wandering afar is not supposed to be sold nearer home." This proverb is used sometimes when a lady known for her flirtation wants to marry. It is expected that nobody around her vicinity will marry her because they know her antecedent. Such woman can only be married by a foreigner who does not know her past.

It could also be used for a troublesome lady.In those days, it was common for some ladies to park their load and return to their father's house at any slightest quarrel with their husbands. Such ladies are expected to be married far off where they will think twice before embarking on coming back home.

Some happenings to us in life are blessings in disguise. We may not fathom them at first but later we may start appreciating why they happened. For instance God's will for man is never attractive at first. It is after sometimes that we start appreciating why such things happened. No wonder it is said that. "The rain that beat the dove has bathed it."

Certain things are not to be contested for. They come naturally at their time. When people start contesting for such things, apart from expending energy for nothing, their action is like rupturing the moral order. Therefore, they will never fail to hear the saying. "You don't contest for kingship." Kings are born but not made. If you don't have blue blood in you, it will be ridiculous for you to start contesting for kingship. In other words, what is for you is for you.

"The clan that kills its king will have few men alive". Kings are not just killed. A king is not expected to die like a fowl. He must put up resistance to any insurgence to his throne. For him to be killed by his clan's men, many heads would have rolled. No strong man surrenders willingly. There must be a fierce fight which will claim several lives.

"And the race for life does not weary anybody." When you are confronted with a problem that wants to claim your life or even threatened your existence, you don't get tired finding a solution to it. You don't mind what it costs you and the miles you have to cover to get the problem solved.

"When an ugly person starts posing it may be mistaken for a struggle from pangs of death." Have you hated somebody before? If yes, you will discover that no matter what the person does to impress, he appears repulsive to you.

"It would be better to remove the monkey's hand

from the pot of soup before it turns into a human hand." It is good to solve problems on time before they get worse. Like said earlier, when an evil practice stays long it appears to be an accepted norm. Truly certain bad behaviours are accepted as conventions today because they have been with us for long. We have ignored them and don't see anything wrong with them any longer.

When an ugly person starts posing it may be mistaken for a struggle from pangs of death.

For instance, giving bribe is a vice that should be condemned. Because it has been practiced for long, if somebody does something for you without collecting something in return, you tend to doubt the genuineness of the favour.

To buttress this point, a lawyer friend traveled from Lagos to Abuja, Nigeria's Federal Capital Territory (FCT) to process a document for his client. At Abuja, one of the staffers at corporate affairs commission assisted him in processing his document in a jiffy without asking for any reward. When he brought the document, my friend was confused whether it was genuine. This is because he was used to people asking him to pay bribe before they can even discuss the issue. It was later he gathered that the man who processed the document for him is a born again Christian.

"Every one lays the claim that the mother's soup is the best". Almost everybody likes self-pride. They say "if you don't blow your trumpet it will rust." You have to be proud of what you have. This is one of the ways of building the spirit of national pride in people. It has to start with the individuals.

People who have plans to deal ruthlessly with others they feel are helpless should better hear this proverbial saying: "When you kill a goat you thought does not belong to anybody, the owner will quickly emerge from the blues."

"If you bite a man on the buttocks without minding faeces, if he is biting you on the head, he will not mind your brain." It is usually good to think twice or be cautious when you want to deal treacherously with others. Before you pinch somebody try and pinch yourself first and see how painful it is. Remember action and reaction are equal and opposite.

Adducing excuse for our misfortunes is very common. In Africa, nobody dies naturally, somebody caused it. This development has caused a lot of bad blood in many families and communities. Perhaps, that is why it is said "anybody flogged by a masquerade must have an excuse why he was flogged".

Many people have more severe problems. But they cover them up and go about with them. However there are others whose problems cannot be hidden. People tend to think that the latter people's problems are the worst. "The man with protruding frontal teeth has the boldest set of teeth," it is said.

Of course, "when sleep becomes sweet, the sleeper starts snoring." Certain events in life demand more participation or involvement because they are becoming interesting. Initially, the events might be painful. But as soon as it becomes sweet or interesting, the participants get more involved. For example if you are promoted into a higher position in an establishment, the tendency is that you will get more involved and committed in the activities of the organization.

Showing affection to people has medicinal effect. Many people who committed suicide or died broken hearted may be due to nobody cared about them. Nobody took interest in their plight. "Merely asking: "How are you? has some therapeutic effect," it is said.

Being left-handed is something people learn when they are small and malleable. There is an age one gets to in life he becomes unteachable. Even the person will not be interested in learning. That is why it is said "you cannot learn to be left-handed in your old age."

"A fool doesn't know that his married sister is a visitor." Women in Africa belong to their husbands' place. Any time anyone visits her birth home, she is welcomed like a visitor. She does not have power in her birth place. Her power is exercised in her husband's house. That is why it is said that the beauty of a woman is the husband. And any woman not married gets alienated and frustrated.

The proverb is used to stress the fact that some

people do not know where to draw the line in some issues. Some people lump up issues together. It would be wrong for a government to mix up its foreign policy with internal affairs.

It is very easy for people to under estimate a small man or small problem. But anyone that does that, it is at his peril. This is because "when you underestimate the small earthen pot on fire, it overflows and puts out the fire." Equally, the stick that blinds a person is usually very small.

Consequently, it is said advisably that "those who can pound, should pound their item inside the mortar. But those who do not know how to pound should Pound on the ground." If you know how to carry out a task, do it well, if you don't know, don't pretend to know. More so, those who have ears should listen to advice.

Valuing what you have is very important. Many people are suffering today because they refused to recognize their God given gifts. Our people said that. "A poor man's fowl is his goat." It is through your eyes that people will see and evaluate what you have. If you rate yourself lowly, people will definitely rate you low. In fact, "If you value your yam seedling, it produces bountiful harvest for you," our elders say.

In the law of inheritance in Africa, when the head of a family dies, the first son inherits a large portion of the property or wealth. Where there is nothing to inherit everybody is equal. But it will be wrong for the burial responsibility to be left for only the first son.

He will be overburdened. Generally, in life who-ever that is rich in the family should help others. It is not compulsory that the first son or the oldest child should be richer than others. Therefore, it is said that "when the father of the house dies, any of the children that is wealthy should bury him because it wasn't the first son that killed him ".

A woman may beget seven sons, they are seven different spirits. The seven are different clans also. Truly no matter how closely related people are, each of them is a legal entity that is bound to carry his cross, his destiny and challenges.

"The unexpected beats even the man of valour". Surprise is one game of life that out wits everybody no matter how strong he might be. If you inform people about what you want to do, the tendency is that they get prepared or take precaution. But if they are taken by surprise, it beats them hollow.

"And anything we don't know is older than us". When you know about a problem or an issue it becomes easy to go about solving it. Where the contrary is the case, you are helpless. It is like a disease that has never been seen before; it cannot be cured with common herbs. So, a peculiar problem requires a peculiar solution.

Fancy yourself being surrounded by enemies. What will you do? You must be very careful with your life or they will devour you. If a man forgets to secure himself before acquiring wealth, the enemy reaps the fruit of the labour." Life is the most precious gift of God. We have to do all within our power to protect ourselves. It is said that when two brothers fight, the enemy benefits. Lack of unity favours the enemy. That is why in warfare, the enemy will always bring in division first amongst brothers so that he can have access to them and destroy them.

My cousin's wife complained bitterly to her friend on how some people she had helped to raise from grass to grace are now fighting her. A lot of them do not want to see her. The friend, a community leader replied with a proverb: "When an orphan develops teeth, he devours the owner."

When people of low means come into positions of authority, they would want to oppress anybody around them. Their air of superiority will know no bounds. It will appear that everybody below them were responsible for their previous misfortunes.

"If a grandchild commits an abomination at the maternal home, the entire village joins forces and push him inside a ditch." Children belong to the society in Africa. Whenever any is found misbehaving, the community disciplines him. This is to prevent anti-social behavior from being part of the child and making him a danger to the society. Generally, society sanctions evil behaviours.

Similarly, "if a little Billy goat starts developing big scrotum from birth, the scrotum will touch the ground." When a little child starts early to learn evil, he would be overwhelmed by it and it will retard his progress. Really the sight of a little child going into organized crime that used to be the exclusives of hardened criminals means such child is bound to die young.

....

If a little Billy goat starts developing big scrotum from childhood, the scrotum will touch the ground.

....

If a little Billy goat starts developing big scrotum from childhood, the scrotum will touch the ground.

Chapter Nineteen

Hese two words above: Thank you, are not easy to come by these days. Many people find it difficult appreciating people for the good they did for them. The two words can be magical when used sincerely.

"If you thank a man for the good, he has done, he will do more." Our society can be a lot better if we can develop an attitude of showing appreciation.

God loves people showing appreciation to him. Our Lord's prayer that contains 64 words (new Living translation bible) started with thanks giving and praise. We are made in the image of God. Therefore, we appreciate thanksgiving too. Practice thanking people for even the smallest thing they did for you and watch how more of such goodies will flow your way.

Praise singing is now a profession in Africa. In many villages and cities, there are young men and women who move from one part of an area to the other like the old Italian Commedia dell'arte, praising people. Most of the people they praise sing acquired wealth illegally. Even some local musicians are skilled in this. Those they praise sing get puffed up and start 'playing god'.

> ***If you thank a man for the good,***
> ***he has done, he will do more.***

An adage has it that "there is an extent you praise a colt it will break a leg in excitement." These men being praised in return spray money on those praising them. But the most agonizing thing is that they get into trouble for sharing God's glory. All glory and honour must be to God for only him is worthy of our praise.

During one of those under 17 World Soccer tournament, all the countries from Africa were eliminated before the semi-final stage except Nigeria. When Nigeria was playing her semi-final match, she was leading by a lone goal and the opponent, Italian squad was very aggressive in attack. The Nigeria radio commentator, Ernest Okonkwo of blessed memory questioned: "Africa would you allow the only palm fruit you have in the fire to get burnt?" However, Nigeria won that match and went ahead to win the competition.

It is not good for one to allow his last chance to slip

by. He must guard it jealously and with all the utmost care it deserves. Such thing does not have replacement.

During my National youth service corps (NYSC) a one year national service programme for all graduates of tertiary institutions with Nigerian nationality, I met a man physically challenged who was part of that year's service at Ondo state, Western Nigeria. The physically challenged man's philosophy was "What you can't get, destroy". What a selfish approach to life?

Another Corper who observed him and his mean philosophy said. "God knows why he gave him one leg. With one leg he is mean. If he had two legs complete, he would have turned the world upside down."

If you pardon the lame corper for being mean, what would you say when you find a man who destroys even what he will benefit from? There are some people who go to the extent of blocking their success or progress; prompting the saying that "it is not good for anyone to spit inside a well he will drink from".

Closely related to this are people who are well off yet the little other people have they want to acquire it. It is a case of greed or self-aggrandizement. Our people say "it is not good for a man carrying an elephant on his head to be digging for cricket with his toes."

If this is pardonable, how would you respond to a case where a man causes a great havoc or offence, he will be directly responsible for its curbing? Does it show any sense? It is often said that "When a man kills somebody he will be directly responsible for the burial rights, does it show the killer is sensible?"

"And when the head dodges from a blow, it falls on the shoulder". Orders in life move from the head down in what has been known in management as the trickling down effect or the pyramid. So, when the head misses in carrying out any responsibility, it falls on the immediate subordinate.

Sometimes, some people feel they have grown so big in a society to the extent that they are immured from any problem. But that is a mere delusion because it is said "No matter how tall a dyke may be,a small hole made by an ant may pull it down". Equally, no matter how tall a dyke may be, ants can climb it.

The latter proverb is closely related to the former. No matter how big one claims to be, when problems come, they can ravish him not minding anything.

The liver and heart are very closely related in the body and perform complementary roles to each other that what affects one some how affects the other. There are people who are so closely related and love each other in such a way that it will be unthinkable for one to harm the other. This prompted the adage that "the liver cannot harm the heart."

"Thought is like goat skin bag; everyone carries his own." In Africa especially amongst the Igbo race of South East Nigeria, male elders who are heads of families go about carrying their goatskin bag on their shoulders which contains several items. A man's thought is like the goat skin bag. Everyone carries his own and only the owner knows what is inside just as it is not easy for anyone to know what's on the mind of the other. Lord

Alfred Denning said even the devil cannot know what is in a man's mind.

Even mad people have friends. "No matter how bad a man maybe he still has friends. There are many people in history like Adolf Hitler, General Sani Abacha, Mobutu Sese Seko, General Idi Amin etc., whom the world condemned as evil. But they had their followers who were ready to die for them.

Of course, a toad does not run in the broad day light for nothing. It is either it is after something or something is after its life. Most of the people accused above had their reasons for acting the way they did.

Their action may be for personal greed or they were suffering from phobia.

For those who cause problems for themselves, there is no need complaining or shifting blame because it is said that "he who collected ants infested faggot should not be offended when lizards visit him". Problems have consequences just as fear has torment. When someone is inviting trouble, what does he expect in return, trouble. For evil begets evil.

"The lion that was looking for whom to devour suddenly finds a prey by his side" Sometimes, out of our carelessness or stupidity some people become prey for the evil one and he does not waste time before consuming them. After all, he does not need to lose sleep or expend much energy before striking.

As a little boy growing up, I noticed that many people from my maternal home were not progressing. There was a high percentage of young men there who were loafers, roaming the village, doing nothing. When I enquired from my father why it is so, he replied me with a proverb: "Your maternal people are like the breadfruit which kills the ground that nourished it to maturity." In other words, he said people from there have the knack for killing those who gave them a helping hand to climb the ladder of life.

However, he tried to adduce an excuse for his in-laws with another proverb that "when another person's corpse is being carried, it appears to strangers as if it is a log of wood. "Explaining that other people tend to ignore what they feel does not affect them directly. He said we could be deluding ourselves because people are related in one way or the other asking "if in an attempt to trick others we trick ourselves, have we succeeded in our plans?"

He emphasized that sometimes many people insist on embarking on a particular action or mission. He buttressed his point with a story of a young man who insisted he would marry a certain lady contrary to advice by many people against the relationship. The young man had his way he said; stressing that "when a child eats what kept him awake in the night, he falls asleep. "Having married the lady the whole trouble was over.

My father, Enoch Ayozieuwa now late said further that many people fail in life because they only prepare for any task when it is too late. He said such people are like the proverbial shrew which makes its nest only when labour pains are close.

He said further that the shrew's case is still alright

because it delivers the babies safely. Sometimes, he added, people are quick to condemn other people's achievements or success. Those who condemn don't really know what it takes to achieve success, stressing that "the tortoise that laughed and mocked the dog because it was stretching the body, should try to stretch its own body." He said there is a level a man will get to in life and he will discover that he needs to chew water before swallowing it.

Upon that, "when an ill-luck man drinks water, it may hang in the teeth", he said." Truly, an ill-luck man usually fails where others have succeeded. Like one elder pointed out in a village meeting arranged to settle dispute between him and his siblings. "When the female anatomy sees me, it develops teeth." What ordinarily is a jolly ride for others may be a lot of pains and problems for an ill-luck person.

***When an ill-luck man drinks
water, it may hang in the teeth.***

My dad advised further that "There is a difference between pregnancy and big stomach caused by constant consumption of beer". In life, he said many things appear the same but one needs to look closely to differentiate the original from the fake.

Being able to differentiate the right from the wrong

is not as easy as people think. It takes a lot of effort and pains. He said that these days they discovered that many young men do not want to be pains-taking. Rather, they prefer violence and deviant behaviour. He said; "when a child is tired of working, he develops raw strength for violence," suggesting that this is an ill wind that does no good to anyone.

"The madman that is dancing by the road side, has his drummer inside the bush." These young men who engage in anti-social behaviours may have support from very important people in the society including some government officials.

These anti-social behaviours he pointed out could have been mitigated if the society fought against them from the beginning. But nobody really showed enough courage to bail the water when it was barely at ankle-deep. "Now the lunatic has ran into the market square, getting healing for him is difficult."

He told us a story about a madman who attended a funeral. The man requested for a plate of rice and chicken, he was offered. He asked for a bottle of cold beer to wash the plate of rice down after eating, he was served. After eating to his satisfaction, he stood up, stretched his body and said "it would be nice if every day will be like today."

When members of the bereaved family heard the madman, they were furious and decided to chase him away. But it is said "Don't argue with a fool for people may not know the difference," of course people were wondering why such respected family members were involved in a row with a lunatic. In fact, many people concluded they were mad for not ignoring the mad man.

Furthermore, he said it was observed that "old fire wood never quenches". The bereaved family is known for their insurgence. It was not surprisingly to many who knew them to conclude that it is in their character. The Leopard will never lose its spots.

As it is said, "when a kola-nut gets home, it tells where it came from". Those who attended the funeral, where the madman caused a row, had a lot of stories to tell when they left.

"The kola-nut says she knows she does not fill the stomach when eaten but she can be a big source of strife amongst people if any one is denied the opportunity of having a portion." Those who attended the funeral and were deprived of getting plastic bowls as take away created some commotion too.

The bereaved family he said were disappointed by such ugly attitude and decided to confront them head-on. "The child that says the mother won't sleep how can he sleep? "They cursed the trouble makers calling them ungrateful fools. The most senior child in the family said "the child carried on the back does not know that the journey was far."

Disappointed by the whole affair, the village head told the head of the bereaved family that the truth is that "the child you are cracking kernel for does not have teeth." Those who were entertained during the burial do not even value the efforts of the entertainers.

One sunny Easter Monday morning, many women from my kindred gathered in our family house. One of my sisters was getting married. As the custom demands, the women will have to cook for our suitors who will come later that day. Preparation for this type of event is usually strenuous and to encourage the women, palm wine is supplied to them to keep them happy.

While other women were busy relishing the drink, my mother who was the celebrant was not drinking. In many African societies when a woman is getting married, during the traditional ceremony the focus is usually on the mother of the bride. You can now imagine why I was surprised that my mother was not drinking. Are you not happy that one of your daughters is getting married this austere time?, I asked her.

She told me that "since she saw the arse of the palm wine taper on top of a palm tree, she lost appetite with his drink." There are people whose life style discourages others from dealing with them or what they do. Some people are just bad public relations for their family, jobs, associations etc.

"When a child is intelligent, he took after the father, when his is a dullard, he resembles his mother."

Nobody wants to associate with a failure. Failure they say is an orphan while success has relations.

"If you continuously maltreat a child, you en-gender strength into him, "this proverb is a reality. According to child psychology experts, the more you use force on a child the tougher he becomes. It is like cheating on somebody. The more you cheat on a person, the more you teach him a lesson and in no distant time, he will learn the tricks and starts cheating on the cheater.

It is only a foolish man that loses what he has before getting another. A bird at hand is worth more in the bush. "Wherever a man gets his livelihood, he guards it jealously "our people say. Have you ever threatened to remove any man from the position that fetches him some goodies? He will fight you with everything within his arsenal. He might even kill if the worst comes.

Some people however waste their time on unprofitable ventures. They become the proverbial man "who washed his hands before cracking kernel for fowls." What an irony? A lot of people expend energy on projects and activities that are unappreciated and unprofitable.

There are others who constitute themselves into an obstacle on other people's progress. They are like a dog in a manger or the biblical Pharisees who will not enter the kingdom of heaven and wouldn't like others to enter. They are said to be like the man who put out the fire a little child brought from the spirit world.

But "the child stung by bees usually flees on sighting a house fly." It is only a fool that allows an evil to happen to him twice. A wise man learns from the first experience. He rejects or fights any second attempt against him that is similar to the first attack or problem.

Have you ever been tortured by a police officer in Africa? If you have, I know the mention of the word police in Africa drives cold blood down your spine and you would wish they never existed. The experience is like being bitten by a snake. "Anyone bitten by snake runs on sighting an earthworm." It is that bad.

"When gifts are given, it is easy to find out who is hated". Most times people manifest their love or hatred for people when gifts are being shared. The loved is easily remembered. Even if he is not present, his share will be reserved for him. But someone hated may not be given his portion even when present.

People tend to argue about who is stronger without really making effort to practically settle the matter. It is often said that "where there is enough space, there is no need arguing about who is stronger." Those arguing should save themselves the energy of arguing unnecessarily by settling the argument practically. At least it is a more reasonable way of resolving such issue.

"A rejected man does not reject himself. "There is a philosophy which says if a man says yes, his personal god says yes. If a man is rejected, he does not need to resign to fate. Rather, he should be strong and confront the problem head-on. After all those who rejected him are not his God. We all have heard and seen people doctors have consigned to the grave yard because of an illness but they recovered. There are people the society never gave the opportunity of succeeding. But with sheer determination and never say-die spirit, they succeeded.

It is said that "the cow without a tail, only the god drives away flies from the body". Those who do not have helpers here on earth get help from above. The Lord said he will help the helpless. If we surrender ourselves to God, he is faithful and just to cleanse us from all unrighteousness. When we can still help ourselves we don't need God. God intervenes when we are helpless and surrender to him completely.

There is a common saying amongst the masses in Nigeria which goes thus: "chop alone, die alone". It is usually used when it is believed that somebody is benefiting from somewhere and does not want to extend the goodies to others. A proverb like this "when a man eats a snake alone, the snake coils in the stomach" is employed to express this feeling.

"And when a child destroys his sleeping mat, he sleeps on the floor." This proverb is a warning to those who may want to destroy their source of comfort or livelihood. There is a big consequence for anyone who destroys his source of livelihood. Hunger and poverty are there to deal a harsh blow on such persons.

When people make a mistake in life, they may have the opportunity of correcting it. Although it is not all mistakes that can be corrected. Some mis takes claim lives instantly. For those who may have another chance, this saying that "when a child goes on a wrong errand, he repeats it" is very appropriate.

....

**_And when a child destroys his
sleeping mat, he sleeps on the floor._**

....

"The entire city jubilates when the godly succeeds,

they shout for joy when the godless dies." This saying reminds one of the death of the maximum Nigerian ruler and dictator, General Sani Abacha. The day it was announced that the dictator was dead, the entire country went wild in jubilation. Many people organized parties to celebrate the sudden demise of a man who held the country spell bound.

In South Africa, it was all jubilation in 1994 when Dr. Nelson Mandela, after being in political incarceration for over 26 years was sworn in as the first black post-apartheid president of the country. Many people believed it was a good case of good succeeding over evil.

He who goes to equity must go with clean hands or he will be disgraced. It is said "the man who calls the police first to a dispute or quarrel is not always the innocent person." In fact it is said that a thief is always the first to call another person thief.

"Success in life is not determined by age." The fact that one is the oldest in a family doesn't translate automatically to success or riches. Success does not just happen they are planned step by step and not according to age. The Wisdom of Solomon has nothing to do with the age of Methuselah. Methuselah lived the longest years on earth according to the Holy Scriptures. But we were not told about his successes.

"A man who blows a flute also blows his nose." Those who serve others also serve themselves. When you are serving people, there are fringe benefits that accrue from it which you will enjoy too. The opposite proverb to this is, "the person looking after a sick person is sick also."

Truly, "when the eyes begin to weep, the nose starts running." Eyes and nose are connected. When the eye is diseased, the nose will not know peace. When a relation or friend is in problem it affects us physically and psychologically.

Similarly, it is said that "There is no way anyone can defecate without urinating. "These two actions go together. They may be likened to the economics jargon of joint demand. It is difficult for one to happen without the other being a witness.

This proverb could be said differently thus: "There is no how the rain will fall without the ground knowing." In other words, nothing is hidden under the sun. There is no action we take either in the dark or within our closet that is not known. We may think they are hidden but one day they will come to the light.

Sometimes we delve into a problem without counting the cost. Many people are known to have paid dearly for taking decisions which they did not weigh the implications. Perhaps that is why it is said "The point one entered a bush is not usually where he comes out from it." Nobody comes out of a problem completely free. No wonder it is said "Don't throw mud for you may miss the target but your hand is stained."

"But no matter how thick a bush may appear; it can be explored". Every problem in life has a solution for those who believe. A peculiar problem requires a peculiar solution. We must not be afraid of finding solution to problems for problems are solved but not evaded.

During the political quagmire in Nigeria after the annulled June 12, 1993 presidential election, all opposition were silenced1. Many were jailed, assassinated and hounded into exile. "It is only a foolish person that can stand in front of a moving train." Those who fought against the inglorious regime attacked from the outside. Eventually, they won with the death of the dictator.

People are advised to be proud of what they do and profess. They should do them with all zeal and equanimity. It does not pay when somebody performs a duty haphazardly. "The man who wants to eat frog should eat a big one so that when he is called frog eater, he will proudly own up".

Sometimes we take irrational decisions in anger which we live to regret later. It is always good to avoid being angry. Anger people say is temporary madness which we must not allow to consume us. Our people say: "If you kill a man in anger you have to bury him in anger."

Of course, the consequences of killing in anger are grave that the killer will not know peace. In an extreme case he may be condemned to death if the Director of public prosecution (DPP) was able to prove that the action was premeditated. If out of provocation it becomes manslaughter whose penalty is equally grave.

"The day a boy threw away palm oil may not be

the day he will be punished. He may be punished on a day he threw away ordinary water." Sometimes people's offences are ignored. On a day they think it does not count any more, it may be used against them.

"A woman whose husband keeps buying meat for, on a day he did not buy any, she will quickly remember the man who would have married her and how nice he was". When a man keeps doing good to people, the day he stops, all his good work will be forgotten and that singular wrong decision he took then will be the only thing remembered. The bible even said this. It means we should not be weary of doing good.

There are many times we inconvenience ourselves because we want to please others. "It is for fear of not offending people that made some people to eat poison." Really, many people have suffered some terrible discomfort simply to please others. It is like swallowing a hot nail because of shame.

"Whatever is scooped from the side of a pot of soup ends up at the side of the mouth", What is got through a fraudulent way does not give satisfaction. It ends in an unpalatable way. This proverb is aimed at discouraging nepotism and fraudulent acquisitions.

Equally, it is said that "when a man blocks his anus, he may not defecate again. "If anyone blocks his source of livelihood either through stupidity, ignorance, or sheer pride, he may starve to death. We are supposed to guard our source of livelihood jealously; making sure that no evil befalls it. Fancy a worker who was privy to a plot to burn down the company where he works and he decides to keep quiet. It means, there will be no job for him to do there anymore.

....

***Whatever is stolen from the side of a
pot ends up at the side of the mouth.***

....

Chapter Twenty

THE TORTOISE IS KNOWN FOR being crafty. A fable has it that a tortoise once approached a native doctor for divination concerning his lost item. While the native doctor was carrying out his divination, he urged the tortoise and the yet to be identified culprit to be attentive.

It takes two to tango. Whereas the man accused is supposed to learn a lesson from being accused, the accuser must also learn a lesson too. The point is that whatever situation one finds himself in life, there is a lesson to learn. The ability to learn from a mistake elevates us into a higher understanding and makes us better people.

Caution is the key word, for "the man who throws stones at the market place, has no assurance that either his mother or father is not there." The abiding advice is for all to shun evil for we can hardly foretell the magnitude of the consequences. A thief is not ashamed of his behavior but his relations are. The perpetrator of an evil may not be affected directly but one of the relations maybe affected.

> ***The man who throws stones
> at the market place, has no
> assurance that either his
> mother or father is not there.***

This reminds of a very famous native doctor who prepared charms for people against their supposedly enemies. One day a lady came to him for a love potion to be given to the lover. He obliged the lady and prepared the portion not knowing that the person it will be given to was the son. The lady gleefully applied it in the food she prepared for the lover but wrongly. The consequence was madness.

When some responsibilities are reserved for some people, no matter what they do, the task is for them. This prompted the saying that "the food in the broken earthen ware is left for no one else except the dog."

One day worshippers in a certain Catholic Church were reprimanding the local priest and threatening that he will be transferred. The priest bluntly told his aggressors that "he was around when the reverend father came and that he will still be around when he leaves".

There are situations in life when you cannot be moved unnecessarily except at your request. It is like moving a military barrack. It is not possible. "Soldiers come and go but barrack still remains."

When problems come sometimes, some people find it difficult tackling them without destroying everything. "It is nice not to throw away the baby with the bath water." You can sieve the problem out without destroying everything.

"If the man who defecated carelessly in the house forgets, the person who parked the excreta does not." When somebody who created a problem forgets about the event, the person who suffered as a result of that problem will never forget. Events will continue to remind him of the problem. It is like a wound on the palm. Even after healing, the scar keeps it fresh in the mind.

Live and let live is a philosophy of living in Africa. This philosophy is responsible for the communal life style of many African societies. It is believed that "When palm wine embarks on a right journey people will drink it and when it goes on a wrong one, it will still be drank." In Africa, you welcome all visitors both good and bad. But for the visitor with evil intention, he will develop a hunch back while going home, it is believed.

People work hard in their youth when their strength can carry them. It is the foundation and things put together that period that they rely on during old age when their strength starts failing. As it is stated in the book of John9, I must work the work of him who sent me while it is day, before the night comes, when no one can work. Even King Solomon pointed out this in Ecclesiastes, chapter 12.

In African, it is said that "the fire wood a man fetched during the dry season, is what he uses to warm himself during the rainy season." It is like Lord Keyne's economics theory of saving for the rainy day.

It is said that "instead the yam seedling being roasted in the fire will stiffen because of insufficient wood, let the fire wood around be exhausted" Sometimes, instead of a situation making bunkum your efforts, you don't mind what it costs you to prevent it from happening. When a challenge becomes an affront to a man's ego, he is ready to employ all the weapons in his arsenal to stop it.

"Do not make a mountain out of a mole". Don't exaggerate a problem. It is not good to make much ado about nothing. Issues should be seen as they are.

"If a man traveling defecates on the bush path he will be confronted by houseflies while returning." When we create problems on our way to the top, we will be hunted by that problem. Life is about sowing and reaping. It is a natural law that respects no one. Anyone who kills to live will have death as sentinel on his door.

If you don't explain to some people their genealogy, there is every likelihood that they will start acting out of the boundary they are entitled to. Thus, it is said that "if you don't tell your slave that he is one, the day his kinsmen visit, he will tell you he wants to go with them."

I remember when my cousin's house girl was acting as if she was the mother of the house until she was made to understand her position. That singular revelation made her change her attitude and finally she absconded from duty.

And "the snake that bit a tortoise has succeeded in biting an empty shell." The tortoise always withdraws into its shell when threatened. Any attack on it is merely on the shell which is like water poured on a rock. It is a waste of time sometimes to expend energy on certain ventures or activities.

Some situations in life are like the tse tse fly which perched on the scrotum. If you allow it to stay there, it will suck you dry and give you the dreaded sleeping sickness (Trypanomiasis). If you try to kill it, if you are not careful you could burst your scrotum and the consequences are grave. Some situations require wisdom and utmost care.

> ***If a man traveling defecates on the bush path he will be confronted by houseflies while returning.***

Oscar Wilde, the Irish playwright, poet and critic once said "I can resist anything except temptation. When he can not resist temptations, what is it then that he was resisting? At times we create situations like this in life. Fancy where a full-fledged man is locked up in a room with a beautiful lady. What do you think will happen? The chances of the two ravishing themselves is over 80 per cent. That is why an adage warned: "You should not keep a goat and yam together."

"The visitor invited to eat is now saying that the host's bolus of foo-foo is bigger than his". Sometimes you bring people into your business or to your home to help them only for the people to start working against you. In some extreme cases, this leads to strife whose extreme consequences could be death.

This development is contrary to the proverbial warning that "a man invited to eat should not eat more than the host."

If God calls you, he will equip you. All the people God called throughout the Holy Scripture, he equipped them to carry out the tasks assigned to them. This same belief is held in Africa where it is said "the god that showed a child yam in a gleaned field will give him the necessary harvesting tool to harvest it?"

"A fowl brought newly into a home usually stands with one leg." This proverb must have been made after careful observations that may have spanned a long time. It is an observation that has to do with behaviours of living things.

When people visit a place for the first time, they tend to comport themselves. After being familiar with the environment, their true self starts manifesting.

The next proverb is also a product of long observation on human behaviour. It could also be said to be one of the proverbs coined out of circumstances observed from a long time. It is said "going to Lagos is not difficult but leaving Lagos is where the problem lies." Lagos used to be the capital city of Nigeria until 1992 when the seat of government moved to Abuja, a Federal Capital Territory (FCT) carved out in 1975 by the late General Murtala Mohammed's government. Currently, Lagos is the commercial nerve of the country.

The city has a lot of pull-on people especially the youths who see it as a place of opportunities. Most people who visited this city not minding it's mind-boggling population but with little working infrastructural facilities find it difficult to leave. In fact, this development gave rise to another saying that: "It will be better made Igbo man not to leave Ajegunle."

Ajegunle is a slum in Lagos. It is a jungle. There is nothing you cannot get there. Many people especially those from the Igbo race of Nigeria settled in that part of the city. Not minding that things are not improving for them, they still stayed put with the hope that one day their situations will improve.

Truly, this is a good example of exercising patience. What sustains life is patience. Just as the people in Lagos and Ajegunle in particular believe it will be well one day, so also many people keep hope alive with the aim that the future is bright.

"If the vulture thinks that growing feathers on the head is easy, let it attempt it for all to see." There are some tasks some people think are easy to achieve. It will be better to allow such people to demonstrate that which they feel is easy to achieve.

Sometimes some people that are being helped want

to help other people when they have not succeeded in their own. This may be seen as foolishness. "A man being carried on the back does not carry another person." This is because the weight of the third person may weigh them down. Two they say is a company. But three is a crowd. This is practical wisdom that does not need too much sermon.

The above proverb is closely related to the maxim that "you first find an escape route before taunting the cobra." It is only a fool who does not weigh his action before taking it. Even the bible urged us to count the cost of our actions, even in following Christ. For any man who did not count the cost of building a house may not finish it.

"When a man who showed a lot of strength initially in a fight now starts throwing sand, know that he is tired." Nobody needs a diviner to tell him that a man does not have an interest in a particular project or programme if the said man showed a lot of enthusiasm at first and later starts slacking. Developing cold feet is a mark of waning interest.

There was this teenage girl in our neighbourhood when we were growing up. She dated almost every man on the street that a song was made in her name. However, she became pregnant and the whole agility and flirtation ceased. One elderly man who lives on the street and was disgusted with the girl's attitude gave this proverb on seeing she was pregnant "the snake and what it swallowed are now lying helplessly on the ground." Honestly, the girl was no more visible and to worsen matters she did not know who was responsible for the pregnancy.

Some sickness sometimes defile medication. Some are incurable. It is said in Africa that the only sickness that responds quickly to drug is hunger. There is this saying that "It would be good if every sickness were to be hunger".

No matter how much the leopard tries, it cannot lose the spots. Africans believe that "No matter what a slave achieved, he cannot become the heir to the throne." You cannot replace legitimacy with illegitimacy. The two don't go together.

"The humility employed by people while trying to borrow money from somebody is not the same employed at time of paying back," This is natural. Most people humble themselves when they want a favour from you, either as gift or borrowing. At time of payment, the language is not the same again. The debtor may even claim that the creditor was insulting him by requesting for his money.

There was a case of a certain rich man who borrowed about $50,000 from a bank. After several years he was unable to pay his debts. When he was confronted, he asked the bank management if they want to insult him because of ordinary $50,000. It was said he was literary begging when asking for the loan. What an irony of life?

"The spray meant for the ears is not good for the eyes". Every problem has its own solution just as every sickness has a drug. When you administer a drug meant for the ears into the eyes you might blind yourself because the components of the drugs are not the same. We have to find out the right approach or remedy for every situation.

"If you don't own something you can't enjoy it whenever you want it. "There is nothing like what belongs to you. You can control how you use it. But when another person lends you anything to use, he takes it when he wants. Perhaps when he wants it is when you probably want to make use of it.

It is not possible for a very rich man to become very poor as to be going cap-in-hand begging people for what to eat. There is a level somebody gets to in life, it becomes difficult for him to fall to the nadir of life when things become difficult. Consequently, it is said "there is no how the cow will emaciate and come to the size of a goat."

Our people say "when a deity misbehaves so much, you show him the stick he was carved from". When somebody who rose from rags to riches starts misbehaving, the people may tell him how his past was. The people of Nigeria sometimes say that they will show Chief Obasanjo, their third elected president how he was before they voted him in as president. Chief was very lean and worn out when he was released from jail and brought forward as a presidential candidate in 1999.

Many people cover their problems. By so doing, they allow such problems to gain ground and become a norm. That is why it is said "when you expose an illness, it leaves you".

"The old gun has turned into a playing toy for the

children". It is said that when an elder makes himself an essential commodity children will buy him. If people lower themselves in esteem, they will definitely be insulted.

"And when a little child speaks several abominations in the night, he thinks the dawn will never come" We all have a way of saying evil about a situation that is yet to come. When such situations eventually come and they are not how we thought, we fall into trouble. Night sometimes serves as cover for people to say and perpetrate evil. But there is nothing said in the dark that will not be made manifest.

Attending to a problem early makes remedy effective. Sometimes we allow problems get hold of us tightly before we start looking for a solution. That is why we are advised that it is better to start searching for the black goat when there is still day light.

You are likely going to be insulted or attacked by somebody who knows you. An outsider may think twice before carrying out such acts on you. Thus, there is a saying that "it is only the siblings of a frog that can kick it on the stomach."

"Learn to put a smiling face on a precarious situation" is the best approach to problems of life. Many people wear their problems. This does not improve situation. It worsens issues because it creates tension and tension does not bring out the best in people.

It is difficult for people to defend effectively what does not belong to them. Whenever a problem arises, anyone who is not the owner of a property tends to chicken out hence confirming the saying hired sheep keeper will always run away when the lion prods on the sheep."

"You don't wink at somebody in the dark." This proverb has been popularized by advertisers. They claim that doing business without advertising is like winking at somebody in the dark. You know what you are doing. Does the person you are winking at know?

It is better most times to know the root of a problem for it helps in providing an early solution. When we lack this common knowledge, we might be wallowing in the dark. No wonder it is said. "Any man who does not know when rain started falling on him may not know when it will stop."

Some people commit crime and expect others to sympathise with them. Crime is an offence against the state and attracts some punishments according to its gravity. This is even more painful when the offence was willful. "For the man who committed suicide should not expect anyone to weep at his burial."

"As a knife being sharpened on a stone is chopping off the stone gradually so also the stone is chopping off the knife." Sometimes when you are cheating on somebody, that person is also cheating on you. It is a kind of not mutual symbiotic existence. It follows the common saying that a cheater must be cheated or the measure you give is what you get.

This reminds me of many young girls who ran after sugar daddies with the believe that they are cheating on the 'old fools', as the are wont to say. But unknown to them, the old fools are also cheating on them. It won't be out of place if they share HIV virus willfully.

....

*Any man who does not know when
rain started falling on him may
not know when it will stop.*

....

Chapter Twenty-One

As a little boy growing up, I noticed that many men older than me in my village were not educated. I was deep in thought about this problem especially when I see men of their age who are top executives in companies in the cities. Each time I asked why they were not educated, the only answer I got is that there was nobody to sponsor their education.

My inquisitive mind made me to inquire from some of my uncles whom I thought were in the Position to mobilise resources together to train one or more of those older men who claimed they never had helpers.

One of my uncles known for his bluntness told me this proverb: "If you climb a good tree, you may be given a push". Furthermore, he asked, did you have anybody to train you? Did you not lose your father during the civil war? But because you are intelligent and promising, help came. Some of the people complaining now that they never had any one to train them were dullards. They never passed their standard six examination. "My pickin, listen to me, anybody that pursues a worthy cause will always get help," he said.

***If you climb a good tree, you
may be given a push.***

Furthermore, he said "pumpkin leaves don't flourish for lovers of vegetables." Sometimes, what you like does not come to you. You have to make effort to grab it. No venture, no success, people say. Therefore, for a man to sit down and complain daily is foolishness.

"An evil laden moon can be easily identified". Evil omens or problems that are ahead give some signs. Sometimes, the signs are very obvious that even children can see them.

Power is an aphrodisiac. It intoxicates and needs handling properly. It is often said that "a child that has the support of the father to steal does not go stealthily, he breaks the door."

"You cannot put a piece of live coal into the palms of a child and ask him to carry it with care". It is practically impossible to expect somebody put in a difficult situation which threatens his life to be calm or quiet. It smacks of wickedness.

Of course, when we see somebody being mal-treated, we should not keep quiet. As pointed out by Nigeria's Nobel Laureate, Professor Wole Soyinka in the novel. The man Died," The man dies who keeps silence in the face of tyranny.

So, "let the slave who sees another being cast into a shallow grave know that he will be buried in same way when his day comes." If an oppressor succeeds in his first efforts, he would want to extend his oppression to others.

"The world is like a mask dance. If you want to see it well you do not stand in one place." Life is full of challenges. We keep on trying everyday to surmount the obstacles on our way. But this is not achieved by staying at one place. We have to move from one point to the other for nobody knows where his fortune lies, the proverb seems to explain.

It would be a great irony for anyone to carry battle to a peace meeting. It will negate the whole effort and ridicule the man who did such thing. It is like the saying that "It is only a foolish man that can carry poison to a purification ceremony." The two things do not go together.

A popular English saying has it that those who live in glass houses should not throw stones. If we know that we do not have the capacity to withstand any problem, we should not attract such problems. Those who wish to act contrarily should better listen to this proverb: "A man who knows his anus is small does not swallow an udara seed". Udara is a berry whose seeds are as big as pebbles. People sometimes swallow the seeds mistakenly. But those with small anus find it difficult defecating after swallowing the udara seed.

"An old woman is never old when it comes to the dance she knows" What we are adept in doing, no matter how bad the condition we find ourselves, when called upon by situations and circumstances to re-enact such things, it does not take us any time. We are always ready to re-enact them. This is an opposite to the saying that the dance learnt in old age, the waist is always stiff to respond.

Expectedly, "the man who sends a child to catch shrew will also give him water to wash his hands." To understand this proverb, it is better we understand what shrew is about. It is a small mouselike animal that leaves an offensive odour on the palm when caught. So, before one embarks on such mission, he has to keep water and soap to wash himself.

Equally, if anybody is sending another to do a dirty job, he must provide what the person will use in cushioning the effect of such effort. No hard or dirty task is embarked upon free. It attracts some payment and usually it is handsome.

It is only a foolish man who can go after a leopard with his bare hand". This proverb is similar to the one immediately before it. The leopard is a dangerous animal. No one should dare to think of approaching it. You can imagine then if one decides to do so with bare hands. It means the person is ready for suicide. For nobody sees a looming danger and decides to confront it.

It is often believed that a stranger always comes with good intensions. Consequently, it is prayed proverbially that "the stranger will not kill his host with his visit, when he goes may he not go with a hunch back." It is also believed that if a stranger comes with bad intensions, he will suffer the consequences while going.

In Africa, "a man may refuse to do what is asked of him but may not refuse to be asked." There are prerogatives in life. Everyone has to exercise that which is due to him. If your respondent replies positively, fine. But if not, you have done yours. And it is not always that you are expected to respond positively as it depends on the content of the demand.

We are expected to trust and believe our father just as we believe God, our almighty father. This is because we know he is loving and can't do us any harm. You can stand by whatever he tells you. This is responsible for the saying that "When a child says while arguing that his father told him he has sworn the greatest oath."

And our people say, "He is a fool who treats his brother worse than a stranger." Blood, they say is thicker than water. And when a corpse starts decomposing even the best of friends leave". There is no way a stranger can be better than the worst brothers.

There are procedures in life. When we do not follow the proper procedures of doing things, we run the risk of jeopardizing our interest or causing harm to ourselves or close ones. "It is better to chase away the wild cat first, before blaming the hen."

Anyone who started a particular trade or business

first is more knowledgeable than a new entrant. He must have passed through the mills and is refined. There are always incidents to attest to the experiences. It could be said "A woman who began cooking before another must have broken more utensils".

There are certain landmark events that no matter what happens, we are not expected to be absent except in very extreme situations that we cannot help it. This is because "a man cannot be too busy to break the first kola nut of the day in his house." For instance, it will be unexplainable if a man alive refuses to partake in the naming ceremony of the first son.

Similarly, our elders say "harmattan greeting is issued from the fire place." Wherever you find yourself in life, no matter the condition, you can still give a helping hand or be friendly from there.

Sometimes when we visit a busy man, we expect so much attention. This is wrong. There are situations and circumstances that make people not to act properly as they should. "A visitor to a craftsman should not expect much attention." You don't expect the person to abandon what he is doing to give you all attention especially when the visit was not official.

When everything fails a man hinges his hope on anything he sees no matter how little and ordinary. Hope sustains life. And where there is hope there is life. For it is said". A man who has nowhere else to place his hand for support puts it on his own knee."

Over familiarity brings insult. As people say in the local parlance too much kissing produces mouth odour.

There are people immediately you start relating with them, they take advantage of you. They are like the proverbial leper who spread out his arms soliciting for an embrace because his host shook his hands.

Certain development nearly put an end prematurely to one of the most hilarious and longest running sitcoms in Nigeria - The New Masquerade. It was originally called "The Masquerade" and created by James Iroha of Nigeria Television Authority (NTA) Aba, now in Abia state. When the programme was made national because of its popularity, the creator was sidelined. He resigned and took the NTA to court. It was decided that as at when he created the programme, he was a staff of the NTA. Therefore, whatever creativity he came out with, the copyright belonged to his employer. Thus, giving credence to the saying that "The owner of a man also owns whatever the person has."

Having a Nigeria Policeman as a friend is one thing many people dread like poison. Whenever you meet any of them you must part with something.

They are like the proverbial masked spirit. "When they visit you, you must appease their footprints with presents."

For those who travel, there is need to listen to this proverb: "A man who travels regularly should avoid making enemies." This proverb could be an advice to all and sundry. As we travel in the journey of life, it is better not to make enemies because the enemy we create on our way may be the person that will help us later in life. Don't throw mud for you may miss the target but your hand is stained.

Any man of wisdom does not get fixated at one stage of life. He progresses with time to the upper part of the ladder of life. Especially, when his mates are achieving greater feat, he does not get satisfied at the lower rung of the ladder. That informed the saying that "only a foolish man that can settle with chasing little bush rodents while the age mates are after big games."

Furthermore, A man without appetite for a food should not discourage others who do. "The rat should endeavour to keep off the road for the tortoise if it cannot run fast enough." There are people who are well endowed in life to make progress fast. When they refuse to utilize their opportunities, they must not constitute obstacles on the way of other people who are not well gifted but want to make progress. There are people who are like the biblical Pharisees that will not enter the Kingdom of God and wouldn't want others to enter.

People of the same village or community may quarrel and kill themselves. But when they meet in the city, they behave as brothers. There are cities you visit; you just want somebody from your country no matter the part he comes from. This inspired the saying that "even a quarrelling clans man is a brother in a foreign land".

Chapter Twenty-Two

THE SUCCESS WE MAKE IN life does not depend on how intelligent or careful we are. It depends on God's mercy. We all have different degrees of mercy. That is why it is not good to join others in doing evil for you don't know the amount of mercy you have. And God is the only one that bestows mercy on man and He does it as it pleases him. We cannot query him.

Therefore, our people say, "when a careful man walks through a market with all the utmost care he can muster and his wrapper pulls a bottle of palm oil and it spills, he is held responsible and not the wrapper."

We might take all the care in the world yet one thing in us brings shame or pulls us down. We are still responsible. We can't tell people it is just that hot temper or wagging tongue, for they are part of us.

"It is also said that a fowl does not eat into the belly

of a goat." Whatever we have belongs to us. We cannot say we are acquiring it for another person.

**It is also said that a fowl does
not eat into the belly of a goat.**

We are responsible for every action we take in life. There is no excuse what so ever.

Many people spend fortune, to enter all sorts of secret cults and pressure groups in order to get recognitions in the society like political appointments or reaching the peak of their profession. But there are still people these things are offered to on a platter of gold and they rejected them. That is different strokes in life. And it is said that "sometimes it is good to spit out a morsel fortune puts in a man's mouth." This might appear foolish to a reprobate mind but the person who did that may command much respect especially now that people just scramble for position, without minding how they get them. If you have not wrestled with one of those who have made your compound their thorough fare, others will not stop." Sometimes we have to stand up and fight for our right or nobody will. Part of the reason why some people are taken for granted is because they remained passive or docile as their integrity got threatened.

Similarly, the man to dread in a battle is the one that is ready to take any type of insults first." Some people's ability to swallow every phlegm for fear of offending others makes nonsense every effort of others to bring about a change. Such people are better avoided in battle or put aside before they weaken others. Such people kill the moral of others.

But "it is not good to clean the anus before passing excrement." There are actions in life that connote foolishness. When the wrong things are done first in life, wrong results are obtained. It is always good to follow the proper procedures of doing things in order to get good results.

Delay could be very dangerous in life. It may rob one an opportunity of getting bigger things done for him. Our elders used to say that the toad lost the opportunity of growing a tail, because he was always saying: I am coming! I am coming!

"Whatever dance step that reigns in a man's time, he learns it." Whatever good thing that is in vogue in your era, you have to be part of it.

When there is a prophecy or policy statement, It is not good to ignore it. Doing that might be expensive in the future. "Only the insane could sometimes approach the menace and mockery in the laughter of deities," our elders say.

There are times we may be asked to do something. Our effort or tactfulness in trying to get a better explanation may worsen the matter. It is good sometimes to make do with what we are told. Our people say radio does not speak twice and that "a god who made a request for a chicken to be sacrificed to him may rather want a goat if asked a second time."

Our elders also say "he whose name is called again and again by those trying in vain to catch a wild bull has something he alone can do to bulls". Truly there are situations in life that a particular person is needed and nobody else. Sometimes we wonder why such person must be the only one needed for such task. May be his style or dexterity in doing that thing singled him out. After all a man's gift makes a way for him says the holy bible.

For people who would want to be ahead of others in anything, it is important for them to hear this word of wisdom, "the man who always walk ahead of his mates may receive the first bullet."

Those who know they are not well endowed to do certain things may decide to act like the bat. The nocturnal mammal says: "he knew he is ugly and chose to fly by night". At least it is a perfect blend. Night will give it cover.

The man on top sees farther than others and any decision he takes may have a far-reaching effect on others. Equally, decisions taken by our representatives have a way of affecting us immensely either positively or negatively. If they take rash decision the people they represent are bound to suffer it. That is why it is said that "when the air is fouled by a man on top of a palm tree the fly is confused."

"Even while people are still talking about the man rat bit to death, Lizard takes money to have his teeth filed." These days, people are worried about their security and global peace, yet many novel ideas are hatched to perpetrate terrorism and breach global peace. Many more youths are warming up to be part of the obnoxious act even with the new strategies various governments are putting in place to alleviate the problems.

"The old woman who rushes to gather the wood of a branch of iroko tree that fell on the ground, why can't she climb the tree and take them and let's see?" People who enjoy certain things because other people have suffered to make them available, if allowed to source for them would they be able? There are many people who wouldn't make effort to do any thing but when they see an already prepared, they pounce on it as if nobody worked for it.

....

***Even while people are still
talking about the man rat bit
to death, Lizard takes money
to have his teeth filed.***

....

There are also many people who live on others. Some people call them hangers on. They are ready to do anything to stay put. They are found mainly around politicians or money bags in Africa. All they are after is what they can get to keep body and soul going on daily. When their bread winner dies, they vamoose. It supports the saying that "When the mighty tree falls, the little birds scatter in the bush." It also reveals that in time of adversity only those who are committed will stay put.

If you are fighting with somebody and you pin him to the ground, you are still holding yourself. It is when you leave the person that you will be free from the pin fall. Therefore, it is said: "The little bird which hops off the ground and lands on an anti-hill may not know it is still on the ground".

Sometimes, we do certain things and think we are free from the consequences, not knowing that we are not. We are still within the purview of the consequences of that incident.

"Anyone who says the sickness suffered by the monkey was not serious should endeavour to see the swollen eyes of the nurse who fanned the log of wood used in keeping the monkey warm." People tend to ignore or belittle other people's plight. Such people need to find out from those who suffered because of the person's misfortune or those who bore the cross with him in order to believe.

When a goat eats palm fronds off of a man's head, an abomination has happened. It is a bad omen and forbidden. So when it is used proverbially that "a goat has eaten palm fronds off a man's head" it is an exclamation of an evil happening.

In Greek mythology it is believed that man is like a pawn on a chess board to be manipulated at will by the gods. Man does not control his destiny. Whatever the gods say is what he does. This belief is still held sacrosanct by many African societies. Hence, it is said that "a man is like a funeral ram which must take whatever beating that comes to it without opening the mouth."

"Nobody sends his son up the palm to gather nuts and then took an axe and felled the tree." To do this is a mark of wickedness and no parent would love to do it. No parent would want to punish the child unnecessarily or see a bad road and ask him to pass through. It is the responsibility of every parent or adult to lead the young ones to the proper path of life.

Sometimes, people embark on worthless ventures or foolish programme. Such exercise in futility only exposes their level of reasoning or intellect. It is like the proverbial saying that "it makes no sense pouring grains of corn into a bag full of holes."

Beyond this, sometimes we embark on some plans with the aim of punishing or shaming others. Like people say in the local parlance, when we are pointing one finger at another person the other four fingers are pointing at us." Similarly, a man who makes troubles for others is also making it for himself.

Why we ask our neighbour to see us off when we visit is not that we don't know our way back. It is the fun of having a neighbour or relation. Truly why we share things with others may not be because they are lacking but because of the spirit of love, sharing and caring. Our elders say: "A man who calls his kinsmen to a feast does not do so to save them from starving."*

"And a clan was like a lizard, if it lost its tail it soon

grew another."* Nature abhors vacuum. And a man's place in a society is not always there waiting for him. If he leaves or is no more, another person takes over. It would be foolhardy for anyone to delude us that nobody will be able to fill our position when we are no more there.

At times, how we behave in a society or group depends on the atmosphere of love existing there. There are places you visit you feel at home and vice-versa. Your body instincts and psychological filters will communicate impulses into your brain if you are not comfortable. That is why a proverb says: "As a man danced so the drums were beaten for him."

Many people believe in the fatalist school of thought's say- ing that 'whatever will be, will be'. Some people are known to resign to fate in life. This is completely wrong. There are so many people who were able to change the fate that awaited them. We know the case of Jacob who wrestled with an angel and refuses to give up until he was blessed. The angel blessed him by changing his name from be ing a supplanter (Jacob) to Israel and he prospered. There was Jabez whose name means sorrow and he suffered all sorts of sorrow until he approach God in prayer to change his name and it was changed and his life became better.

***As a man danced so the drums
were beaten for him.***

There are many people in our present day existence who have been able to change the course of their life through perseverance, doggedness and trust in God. Therefore, "to lie down and resign to fate is madness."

214

Chapter Twenty-Three

N MY FIRST YEAR AT the University of Calabar, I was stunned by the heated level of campus politics that I met. First year students were swarmed by a bee of older students campaigning and seeking for elective positions. The new Arts Theatre, venue for our General Studies courses was a theatre indeed for these student politicians to approach a large percentage of the new students under one roof and to tell us what positions they were contesting for and what they would do if voted in.

There was among these political gladiators, a particular one who was never liked by many young students, perhaps because of his physical looks. Each time he mounted the stage to introduce himself and explain the post he was running for, he was shouted down, using such campus dismissive phrase *ewu* politics -(political goat in Igbo language).

One day when we were shouting on this very campaigner, he stood his ground and replied as loudly as he could; "Even if the future does not look rosy, to resign oneself to the situation is to be crippled fast. I will continue to disturb you until you give me your mandate". That was an impressive testimony to the spirit of never-say-die. Many people resign to fate easily when confronted with problems forgetting that most good things are clothed as problems. Whatever you love and cherish, you preserve it and it lasts for you. If you appreciate what you have it works for you. The saying is there that "kola nut lasts long in the mouth of those who value it".

"Happiness has a slender body that breaks easily." Good things we know appear fragile in that they don't last long. They are supposed to be nurtured and carefully preserved. Like it is said, money doesn't stay at a place; so also happiness doesn't stay in one place. It roves about.

When one of the prominent politicians died in Nigeria some time ago, his son was asked: "Now that your father has achieved so much and it is often said that a child should achieve more than the father, do you believe you can surpass your father's achievements?". The young man looked up for some time as if plucking the answer from above and said: "I will step into my father's shoe" His father's shoe is surely too bogus for him, he had to mend it to his size as latter day events showed. However, the good thing was that the man was able to define his path as the new head.

Truly, a vacuum seems to exist in that family today

thus supporting the saying that "When the head of a household dies, the house becomes an empty shell." Moreso, there are many organizations and bodies where the centre cannot hold today because of the demise of the head and founder.

> ***Even if the future does not look rosy, to resign oneself is to be crippled fast.***

There is a saying that "If you like, take a monkey to London, monkey must always be monkey." There are people, no matter what you do to them, you cannot change their behaviour or approach to life They remain what they are. This confirms the saying that "when rain falls on the leopard, it does not wash off its spots."

Most problems that destroy people or institutions start from within and persistently eat deeply and steadily like cancer. Many corrupt societies of today, did not just become corrupt overnight. It is something that has been inside the people and going on gradually over a long period. "The ruin of a land and its peoples begins in their homes."

We often resort to running from pillar to posts when we have problems. Most times, in attempt to get solution outside we put ourselves into more problems.

We find it difficult to do self-appraisal to find out the cause of our problems. In fact, it is very easy to blame outsiders for our woes.

Like Sigmund Freud pointed out, that most marital problems begin from the marriage bed. In other words, most causes of such problems are internal. Therefore, it is important we look inward when we have problems than outward. It must be stressed that "If you need help, search for it first among your selves." You have to do something before expecting others to assist you.

"Can there be anything private about a whole kingdom in pain?", our elders say. When you are overwhelmed by problem and it is known by many already, there is nothing private about it. It becomes the pain of many who care to share in it.

There is always executive responsibility for the head of any organization or group. If the organization is succeeding, he takes the praise and if it is failing, he takes all the bashings. He is at the helms. It is often said that "the secret of a home should be known first to the head of the home." Because of the influence the head wields he is expected to know first any developments.

No matter how much some people try to distinguish themselves from their group or type, they are still what they are. It is often funny when many people from Africa try to align with other parts of the world because they don't want to be seen as Africans. The truth is that in the eyes of the West, we are all Africans no matter how much we pretend. Whatever standard used in judging Africans will be used for such people. For, "a cooking pot for the chameleon is a cooking pot for the lizard," our people say.

"The horns cannot be too heavy for the head of the cow that must bear them". God is a perfect creator. He made us all in wonderful ways. Whatever responsibility that comes our way, God knows we are able to carry such because he had already made provisions for us. However, only those who have 'eyes' are able to see the provisions made. Even the bible said that God cannot give us any temptation we cannot carry because he knows our weaknesses.

However, we must tread carefully in life. Life is precious and must be guarded jealously. It is the only precious thing we have. Whatever that is done to preserve life is more than life itself. If you do not protect your life, it will be extinguished when it is not time. "If you leave your pot unwatched in the fire, it will burn", is a proverb that attests to this.

Injustice is the bane of every society. It is the root cause of all the problems that we all are going through in the world today. It comes in different forms, shades and colours. "Until the rotten tooth is pulled out, the mouth must chew with caution."

Sometimes we use other people as guinea pigs in life and we tend to take precaution from their plight. "When the frog in front falls into a pit, others behind take caution."

We are often advised not to argue with a fool for people may not notice the difference. When we encourage people to do evil, we are also involved in the evil because "he that drums for a sick man, is sick himself ".

It is believed in Africa that if you did not offend somebody no matter what evil he does to you, he will not succeed. He may appear to be gaining ground initially but God will not allow evil to triumph over good for there is always poetic justice. So, "when the evil plotter beats his drum for the down fall of the innocent, the gods will not let their drum sound."

There are people who romance with their enemies not knowing that their death is at hand. Most times I pity young girls who go out with total male strangers in the name of trying to enjoy themselves. The result of most of such relationships is grave. It is like the proverbial saying that "the hyena flirts with the hen, the hen is happy, not knowing that her death has come".

Until the rotten tooth is pulled out,
the mouth must chew with caution.

And of course, "two rams cannot drink from the same bucket at the same time." The result will be fierce fighting and destruction of the bucket and water. Two arch-enemies cannot co-exist together. They will tear themselves into pieces.

The bible says everybody's faith will be tested. And the only way to know a man is when he is tested. Like

Sophocles said in the Greek tragic play 'Oedipus Rex', "And none can be called happy until that day when he carries his happiness down to the grave in peace. We can only beat our chest that we are successful when we have overcome every test. "For meat that has fat will prove it by the heat of fire"

"Because the farm owner is slow to catch the thief, the thief calls him thief. "If we don't nip a problem in the bud, the problem may grow into a Frankenstein monster and challenge us. There are people whose slaves have risen up against them because they did not make them understand who they are.

The strongman can only manifest his power where the weak are. He cannot challenge those who are stronger than him because any attempt to do that will be futile. It is like the saying that "No termite ever boasts of devouring a rock."

One of Isaac Newton's laws of motion proves that nothing happens for nothing. For every cause there is an effect. "Trees and bushes only sway sideways when the wind blows."

There are certain situations in life we find ourselves, no matter how we try to change them it is an effort in futility. So, all we have to do is to appreciate such situations instead of allowing them to weigh us down. "For the snail may try, but it cannot cast off its shell."

Uniquely, there are things you don't just know about except you devote time for them. For instance, when we were in secondary school, we were told that the secret to knowing the sciences especially mathematics, physics and chemistry was devoting more time to them. "Secrets of the owl must not be known in the daylight" our elders say.

Consequently, "the clan where people are quick to inherit ancient family stead, members are not interested in the recovery of the sick." Truly, in any place where people are quick to appropriate a dead man's property, they pray for death to visit one another because they believe such situation will enhance the life of the living. This is a dangerous attitude because it will lead to people eliminating each other.

When you are fighting a right course, it is difficult to get tired. You might get all the discouragement but your strength will not fail you because you know where you are heading to. This attests to the saying that "it is impossible to develop eyestrain from looking on the bright side of things.

Success in life is not about your size. The movie "The Lord of the Rings" tells us a perfect example that success in life does not depend on size. In fact, we are as big as we think in our heart. We might be a pint size but with a mountain size of heart. No wonder the saying that "Even the smallest person can change the course of the future."**

But one thing we must avoid doing is betraying trust. Nothing destroys people like betrayal of trust. It has destroyed many politicians, businessmen and pastors.

Betrayal of trust is like the proverbial "Dog that ate the bone that was hung on the neck."

This proverb is one of those coined after the arrival of Western education. It is used to explain a situation where people's expectations from you over an issue are high. For instance, people might expect that you should know about a particular issue or subject by hindsight or by virtue of your background.

For such people, this proverb "It is not everyone that lives on school road that attended school" is apt. It is often said that those who live closer to churches attend service late. This is akin to the school proverb.

"Fish starts decaying process from the head side. "This is a maxim which elucidates that things start getting wrong in organizations or families from the head. Why at every point in life there are leaders is to ensure that things work. Any organization where things are not working, look towards the leadership. There must be leadership problem in it. Good leadership begets good followership. When the head knows what he is doing, the other parts of the body will fall in line. The followers can often be swayed to fall into line when the head is good. Show me an efficient head and I will show you an efficient organization.

***

Even the smallest person can change the course of the future.

PART 3

Proverbs at a Glance

- When an evil practice stays long it becomes a tradition.
- You don't avoid battle because of fear of being killed in it.
- It does no good to charm a snake after it has bitten already.
- If the dog has bitten already driving it away is not important.
- When a little boy carries his father up, the father's wrapper blindfolds him.
- Whoever that sees a fowl scattering faeces with the legs should drive it away for no one knows who will eat its legs when it has been turned into meat.
- A penis that did not die young will eat bearded meat.
- A man who is fidgeting while sleeping with a widow does it mean he does not know where her husband is?
- If a boy did not grow into maturity before probing what killed the father, he runs the risk of being killed by the same thing.
- Nobody can foretell the womb that will give birth to a king.

- Nobody can hide pregnancy. When an evil becomes too much, people point at it.
- There is an extent a King will be respected after which someone will veil himself to challenge him.
- You cannot cross a log of wood with both legs at the same time.
- When a nursing mother spoiling for a fight sees somebody she can beat, she quickly requests that somebody should help her carry her baby.
  But when she sees one that can beat her, she will quickly say: If not this baby I'm carrying..
- When a pledge is made with an empty hand, the days pass by quickly.
- A short man who takes offence because he was told he is short, will he grow over night?
- A palm wine taper cannot explain to people all he sees from the top of the palm tree.
- Anyone not present when a corpse was buried usually starts excavation from the leg side of the grave.
- Death advises everybody not to forget him when making future plans.
- A planned battle does not consume even the cripple.
- There is nothing you can do for a lame person without him exposing his buttocks to you while leaving.
- The same thing applies to a bicycle rider, he must show you his buttocks too.
- When one finger touches oil, it soils others.
- A woman with big buttocks will know the gravity

of the weight she is carrying when there is a race to be run.

- Being tall is not a sign of maturity.
- No matter how tall an okra tree may grow, it can not be taller than the person that planted it.
- When a road is good, it encourages people to use it more often.
- If at anytime an arrow is fired it hits at a particular spot, does it mean the arrow was made for that spot?
- A well traveled child is more knowledgeable than a grey haired elder in the village.
- If you look at a King's mouth, you may think he never sucked his mother's breast.
- A man does not stop sucking breast.
- A man who never believed he can take an Ozo title usually ties the Ozo bangles round his legs and arms after the ceremony.
- Let the kite perch, let the eagle perch. Anyone that says the other should not perch should show him where to perch.
- Those whose palm kernels have been cracked for them by benevolent spirits should not forget to be humble.
- When a man becomes successful where others failed he thinks he is cleverer than the others.
- Anyone who begins a race before God will run without an end.
- Nobody can clap with one hand.
- When the right palm washes the left and the left washes the right both of them become clean.

- You can not make omelette without breaking egg.
- Laughter does not push anyone to the ground.
- Laughter does not connote happiness.
- It is only a tree you will inform that you will uproot it tomorrow and it will still be there waiting for you.
- Any thought that resulted into murder was not done on impulse, it must have passed thought through the night.
- If you are carrying me on your back and my legs are touching the ground, it will be better if you allow me to walk with my legs.
- When the moon is in its full course, even the cripple get hungry of walking.
- The sun will first shine on those standing before shinning on those sitting.
- Eke Atta market says, it's yet to see all the market people standing, not to talk of those sitting
- The dog says why he loves following a man with big stomach is that, if the man does not defecate, he may vomit.
- The male vulture says, he is not disturbed by the eggs the female vulture is hatching, in that if she hatches them successfully, it is good and if unsuccessful it is also good.
- The snake seen by one person is usually as long as the python.
- When a child washes his hands clean, he dines with the elders.
- A very kind hearted wife is usually maltreated by the husband's relations.

- A woman who sells *'ogiri* can easily tell which housefly that is blind.
- *Eneke-nti-oba* the bird says, since men have learnt to shoot without missing that he has learnt to fly without perching.
- Too much kissing produces mouth odour.
- When a goat that eats no yam starts keeping company with another that eats yam, the former will learn to eat yam.
- It is with a smooth tongue that the snail uses to crawl on a thorny stick.
- If an in-law is not rich, he should at least have sweet tongue.
- There is an extent a man will visit his in-laws, one day he will be told to go into the bush and get forage for goats.
- If a blind man misses the *udara* he found with his legs, nobody will give him another.
- It is better to execute a plan quickly in order to prevent obstacles.
- It is not good to be hasty in licking your fingers because they will not be hanged on the rafters.
- When cloud gathers, the man with a leaking roof becomes restless.
- When dry bones are mentioned in a proverb, an old woman becomes edgy.
- There is no way you can wash an old woman's wrapper without seeing particles of mess. When a woman gets old, it appears as if no bride price was paid on her.

- Anyone that bears a child that steals fowls usually dies of hypertension.
- When a corpse starts smelling, even the best of friends will go.
- When handshake passes the elbow, it becomes an arrest.
- When a situation starts getting tough, it is coming to its end.
- When the penis wants sex it behaves as if it will pull down a house.
- When a man abuses sex, he will realize that the female anatomy takes vengeance.
- Mother bed-bug advised the little ones not to be bothered by the heat they are experiencing because whatever that is hot will eventually get cold.
- It is not good for anyone to hastily lick his fingers during a meal because he wasn't going to hung them on the rafters of a roof.
- When you see a bird dancing by the road side, be rest assured that the drummer is somewhere inside the bush.
- If a rat follows the lizard to run in the rain, if the body of the lizard gets dried will that of the rat also dry?
- As a man is, so also is his problem.
- No matter the cure given to a mad man, he must continue to murmur.
- You can only tell a blind man there is no oil in the soup but not salt and pepper.

- You can foretell the taste of a man's faces by the smell of the fart.
- The antelope says he does not blame the hunter that shot him but the man who pointed him out to the hunter.
- A mad dog has not seen a mad fox.
- It is improper to over feed your baby simply because you believe he is the incarnate of your father.
- It is not good to be carried away by the excitement derived from sex at the peril of the foetus.
- If you want to have friends you should be friendly yourself.
- The anus told the female anatomy that if he knew she will be receiving a lot of visitors, he would not have accepted her as a neighbour.
- You can not judge how bad a market day will be by looking at the early morning deliberations at the market square.
- When darkness comes, it appears as if there will be no dawn.
- The coward holds his life and that of the brave.
- Failure is not a crime but an aspiration to do better.
- No matter how little a deity may be, you must carry it with two hands.
- The rat should not attempt ripping open the native doctor's goatskin bag and the native doctor should not roast the rat's mouth on the fire wilfully.
- It is the mouse at home that informed the bush mouse that there is meat in the kitchen.

- Whatever that is eating up the vegetable is inside the vegetable.
- If there is no crack in the wall, the lizard cannot enter inside.
- Wrinkles don't harm the anus.
- There is nothing new the eyes will see now and cry out blood.
- The swift legs are monitored by the eagled eyes
- The millipede whose head was crushed did not complain rather the man that matched it with his legs is complaining that it has soiled the legs.
- A man with a running stomach does not know a sacred bush.
- When a native doctor lacks the power to heal a patient, he will ask the relations of the sick to bring the eyes of an ant to prepare a concoction.
- It is money that makes a palatable soup.
- The way the bitter kola sounds in the mouth when chewed is not exactly how it tastes.
- The man with a good genital does not appreciate what the other person suffering from the elephantiasis of the scrotum is passing through. You can tell of a ripe maize by looking at it.
- When a snake swallows another, the tail of the swallowed snake protrudes out of the mouth of the one that swallowed it.
- The woman said to rule the husband, does she also stay permanently on top when they are making love?
- When two quarrelling brothers come out of a peace

meeting smiling you can be sure they have told themselves lies.

- When the wind blows we shall see the rump of the fowl.
- When the wind blows, you will notice that reverend fathers also wear trousers.
- . What the dog saw and was barking, the sheep has seen it a long time ago and kept quiet.
- It is after we are through tracing our relationship from the mother's side that we begin tracing it from our father's angle.
- There is no how it will rain without the ground knowing.
- A man invited to eat should not eat more than the host.
- A sweet food also inflicts pains on the anus.
- When faced with the choice of choosing between a cow and road, it is better to choose a road.
- Whatever that goes up must come down except
- age. If you impregnate a woman standing, she delivers a mad baby.
- When a little child gets a bad push, he releases a bad curse.
- When a child jumps an elder to make a choice of items in the family, when death comes it will jump the elder and take the child.
- When a decision is taken behind a strong man, it will be nullified.
- A man who loves asking questions will never miss his way.

- The crab says when joke gets to the point of tying the hands behind it is no more interesting.

- Any type of drum you beat in a wealthy man's house, you must find someone that can dance to the rhythm.

- The Billy goat says: Though a lead is tied to his neck and he is being dragged to the market square to be sold, but when you look at the chin, you will notice he is a guy.

- The chicken carried away by a kite says she is not crying because what is holding her will leave her, but it is for the world to hear her voice.

- The tortoise being taken away by the captor begged to be dropped on the ground for few seconds. It subsequently scattered leaves around, uprooted trees and shrubs. When asked why he did that he said, at least anyone that comes around will know that he didn't just surrender easily.

- The Billy goat complained that he didn't like what he saw at a funeral ceremony. He said that he observed that when funeral ceremony reaches its apogee, there will be a demand for the Billy goat to be slaughtered.

- It is not good to abandon where people are taking Ozo title for where they are sacrificing to idols.

- When the fowl fouls the air, the ground pursues it away.

- A man whose name is not good for whistling should not allow his name to be whistled with.

- . The man killed by train is deaf.

- Death does not exterminate a clan but foolishness does.
- Death does not know who is a king.
- A man who killed the native doctor that prepares charms for him, does it mean his enemies are no more?
- A child that cries so much does not make it easy for people to know when he has been smacked.
- Whenever a child is crying and pointing at a place, it is either the father is there or the mother.
- The appearance of mechanics does not make it easy for people to differentiate them from mad men.
- Money is the only visitor that deserves to be crippled.
- When a tree falls to the ground, even a woman can climb it.
- When a child stealthily pinches you, you equally stealthily pinch him.
- The ants are never over burdened by load.
- When men urinate together it produces foam.
- The family being fought for should also make effort to stand.
- When you give a child a big gift he enquires who he is to share it with.
- Mother monkey says, she can only vouchsafe for the children in the womb, as for those already delivered she cannot guarantee their loyalty.
- A man who does not ask question before eating any food may one day eat poison.
- If you are not carrying any burden you can't be over burdened by any.

- The woodpecker boasted that when the father will die, he will peck the best wood. Unfortunately for him, when the father died, he developed a boil on his beak.
- A man who does not know how to write, does it mean he does not know how to cancel too.
- When the he goat hides inside a house and the odour fouls the outside has he hidden?
- It is with utmost care that we can lick hot pepper soup.
- The dance step learned at old age is usually stiff.
- When a woman that claims she does not eat rat meat then shares it with the teeth amongst the children, has she not eaten it?
- .If a man starts an evil practice by cheating on vou, he will not stop it with you.
- When you marry an ugly woman and live happily with her, with time, you start seeing beauty in ugliness.
- When a woman pleases the husband, whatever anyone is complaining about is sheer waste of time.
- A wife that reports to the husband every happening around will never be hated by the husband.
- The size of any man's eyes does not determine how far he sees things.
- It is not compulsory that the dead body must be buried in the grave.
- You cannot see a newly born baby's first set of teeth with an empty hand.
- Tears do not blind eyes.

- The grave is always yearning for more corpses.
- You can't tell whether the tortoise is in its youth or it is old.
- If you throw a man on the ground and hold onto him, you are still holding yourself.
- It is not wise to stand afar and start kicking somebody.
- Too much blabbing is not expected in an evening church worship
- The housefly that never listens to advice usually perches on a casket and it is covered with sand.
- As you make your bed, so will you lie on it.
- A woman cannot place more than her leg on the husband.
- The mouse has bled according to the size.
- It is bad for a man to act like the Billy goat which slept with both mother and daughter.
- The gorilla says that fire is beautiful but does not allow anyone to cuddle it.
- The sickness that killed a man must be buried with the man.
- Whenever everybody is included when a booty is being shared, envy is eliminated.
- Killing a wealthy man is better than disgracing him.
- Every animal that has a route must follow its own route. Those without route must move in the wild.
- A woman that keeps harassing the male folks, does it mean she will sex herself?
- You can only show one to his relation not a friend.

- The dog says that "when he falls for you and you fall for him it is all play".
- The fowl does not forget who pulled the tail feather during the rainy season.
- When we seek wealth and forget to secure our lives, the enemy reaps the benefit.
- If the first son in a family does not behave like a lunatic the father will not marry for him.
- When your people marry for you, will they also help you put the sleeping mat for you and your wife?
- Leave whatever that is written on a vehicle and board it.
- If we start shooting the lizard from how it posed on the wall, we may exhaust our bullet.
- When a child is tired of work he develops extra ordinary strength for fighting.
- Old fire wood does not quench.
- If the lizard abandons the Iroko tree, its predator apprehends it.
- No matter how high the termite may fly it will still fall for the frogs.
- The mad man on the road says he knows what he is doing but he does not know what is happening to him.
- When a mad man ventures into the market square, the chances of curing him becomes remote.
- A mad man attended a funeral, he was offered a plate of rice and a bottle of beer. After consuming everything, he stood up stretched his body and said. "It will be nice if everyday will be like today."

- The lizard that fell down from an Iroko tree looked left and right, shook the head and said "if no one deems it right to praise him, he will praise himself."
- All the lizards lying down, nobody knows which one has belly ache.
- When the lion becomes lame, even an antelope can confront him.
- Kinsmen are strength to any man.
- When a woman passes the stage when people ask whose daughter is this, she enters the stage of whose wife is this?
- The beauty of a woman is the husband.
- When a harlot starts ageing, she claims she is being disturbed by mermaid spirit.
- It his not only a dead person whose neck needs straightening, those of the living also needs it.
- A fowl with high tendency of wandering is never sold to someone living nearer home.
- The rain that fell on the dove has bathed it.
- The clan that killed their king can hardly have many men alive.
- Kings are born not made.
- No one gets tired when confronted with the race for survival.
- All fingers are not equal.
- When an ugly woman starts posing it appears as if she is struggling with pangs of death.
- It is better to quickly remove the hand of the

monkey from the pot of soup before it turns into a human hand.

- The parcel that will be opened does not need to be pinched.
- Everyone lays claim that the mother's soup is the best.
- When a stone hangs in the air, every clay pot is greatly threatened.
- When a dog runs into a forest with a bag dangling on the neck be rest assured that all the faeces inside the forest is not safe.
- When a beautiful woman offends she may not be punished but the same does not apply to an ugly woman.
- When you kill a goat you thought is not owned by anyone, the owner emerges from the blues.
- Anybody flogged by a masquerade must have an excuse.
- The man with the protruding teeth has the boldest set of teeth.
- If you bite someone on the buttocks without minding faces, if he is biting you on the head he may not mind your brain.
- Truth is as stiff as a raised penis.
- No matter the gift a child gives to the mother, it cannot compensate for the breast milk he sucked.
- When sleep becomes sweet, we start snoring.
- No man can out give God.
- Merely enquiring about somebody's state of health is therapeutic

- It is not easy to learn how to use the left hand at old age
- A foolish man does not know that the elder sister is a visitor.
- When an elder in the village sees a looming danger and refuses to speak out, when death comes, it will claim the life of the elder first. But if he speaks and the young ones refused to listen to him, death will claim them instead.
- But if he sees it and speak out and the young ones refuse to listen to him, when death comes, it will leave the elder and claim the young ones.
- When you respect an elder you may grow to become one.
- When a man changes style in a marriage, the wife also changes style. In a family, everyone cannot be mad at the same time.
- The wealth begotten by one person is no wealth.
- Death that is awaiting all does not elicit fear.
- When a little child learns how to climb objects, the mother also learns how to shout
- When we under estimate the small earthen pot on fire, it quenches the fire.
- Those who know how to pound must pound in the mortar while those who do not know must pound on the ground.
- The Shrew taunted the mouse asking: "As you are an elder in your clan and still very petit, how does little children look?" The mouse in response asked the

Shrew thus: "As you are alive and smelling awfully how does your dead ones smell?"

- The gadfly says instead it will take insults, let its entire race be exterminated.
- A poor man's fowl is his goat.
- If you hold your little yam seedling in high esteem, it will produce four tubers of yam for you.
- Every pleasant and unpleasant talk enters the ears.
- It is an abomination for an elder to be at home while a goat tethered to a stick delivers.
- When an elder lowers himself in esteem, he receives insults from even the smallest child.
- When the head of the house dies, any of the sons that is wealthy should bury him because it wasn't the first son that killed him.
- Though a man may beget seven sons, what he has is seven clans.
- And though a woman may beget seven children, they are seven different spirits.
- An elder in a family does not speak with all sides of his mouth.
- It is the person very close to the mouth that knows how it smells.
- Sometimes it is good to count your teeth with your tongue.
- When you advice the ear and it refuses to listen, whenever the head is amputated it must accompany it.
- Water does not have enemy.
- Surprise even beats the man of valour.

- No matter how beautiful a girl may be, the father cannot marry her.
- Whatever you don't know is older than you.
- Anyone surrounded by enemies guards his life jealously.
- He that oppresses the poor oppresses his God.
- When somebody visits you and you see him off it's just fun because the visitor can find his way to his house.
- Spirits of the dead are also afraid of the living that's why they choose to come out in the night.
- When an orphan develops teeth he devours the guardian.
- When a grandchild commits an abomination, the entire clan joins forces and push him inside a pit.
- It is not good for anyone to allow his only yam seedling to burn in the fire.
- When a small Billy goat starts early to develop big scrotum, the scrotum will touch the ground.
- When you over praise a colt, it breaks the leg in gyration.
- When you thank a man for the good he has done, he will do another one.
- It is not good for anyone to spit inside a well he will drink from.
- A man carrying an elephant on his head is not expected to be scouting for an ant with the toes.
- When a man kills somebody he will be responsible for the burial, has he really killed anybody?
- When the head dodges a blow, the shoulder carries it.

- The liver and heart are too close to issue threat to one another.
- The tongue and teeth are too close to litigate.
- A man's thought is like the goatskin bag each person carries his own about.
- No matter how mad someone may be he will still have a friend.
- A child that may be prominent may be identified from the beginning.
- A toad does not run in the broad day light without something being after its life or the toad being after something.
- The man who collected ants infested faggots should not be annoyed when visited by lizards.
- The head that intruded into the bees wasp will be stung.
- The lion that was looking for a game to eat suddenly found an antelope at his back.
- When a man says yes, his personal god says yes too.
- It is not advisable for any man to be like the breadfruit which fell on the ground that nurtured it.
- If the hen leaves chom! (noise it makes while in search of food with the chicks), who will give her what she will use in feeding the little ones.
- When people see a strange corpse being carried, it looks as if it is a trunk of dry wood.
- When the village gong sounds, there must be a revelation.
- If in attempt to trick another person, you tricked yourself, have you succeeded in achieving anything?

- When a little child eats what made him keep vigil he quickly falls asleep.
- It is not advisable for anyone to be like the shrew that makes its nest just before labour pains.
- If gold should rust what will iron do?
- If the tortoise says stretching of the body is an easy task let him try it.
- It is a thief that first calls another thief.
- There is a level one gets in life, he will know that he has to chew water first before swallowing it.
- When an ill-luck man drinks water it hangs in his teeth.
- Whatever that bits a dog to death is very strong.
- The strength exercised only at home is no strength
- It is not compulsory that all he-goats must develop horn.
- What killed mother dog will not allow the puppies to grow up.
- If you respect an elder, you will grow up into old age.
- The ant says roasting it in the fire is not the problem but bringing it out of fire
- There is a difference between pregnancy and bloated stomach caused by too much consumption of beer (beer belly).
- When a child is tired of working he develops an extra ordinary strength for fight.
- It is not good to leave the anus that farted to crack the head.
- When kolanut gets home it explains where it came from.

- The kolanut says it knows it does not fill the stomach but can be a big source of strife if anybody is refused the opportunity of chewing it.
- The kolanut has legs.
  The baby that says the mother will not sleep will not sleep too.
- The child carried on the back does not know that the journey is far.
- The child you are cracking kernel for does not have teeth.
- When a child is intelligent, he takes after the father, but when he is a dullard he is said to resemble the mother.
- If you continuously maltreat a child, you engender strength in him.
- A man will always guide jealously wherever he gets his source of livelihood.
- If a woman understands the husband very well, it appears she has given him love portion.
- He who eats the scrotum of a ram is indebted to elephantiasis of the scrotum.
- Being the first born in a family is not a guarantee that one will be the first to succeed in life.
- If not for Satan's temptations, there is no need for a man to be excited over a woman's arse.
- The man who blows a trumpet also blows his nose.
- When the eyes start weeping, the nose begins running.
  You first find an escape route before taunting the cobra.

- It is hardly possible to defecate without urinating.
- There is no flesh found in a dog's head.
- The dog is a cheerful animal even unto death.
- A newly worn pant elicits urine.
- A man whose wife delivered and he claims she took him by surprise, does it mean that nine months was not an enough notice?
- A foolish man will never know when he is insulted.
- The chorus that our village people are returnin from the market, does it actually include your sibling?
- Any one who does not have shame is not fit to live.
- Sandy fingers brought about sandy mouth.
- Any one who does not know the boundary between their farmland and others usually starts clearing their portion from the boundary.
- The point a man entered a thick bush is not usually the point he comes out from it.
- No matter how thick a bush may appear it can be explored.
- It is foolishness to stand in front of a moving train.
- Anyone eating frog should eat one that is fat, so that when he is accused of eating frog he will proudly own up.
- The udara tree says she is not the only one that begets an offspring whose mouth is always squeezed.
- Wherever a motorist can get, a pedestrian can get there too, it is just a matter of time.
- If you kill a man in annoyance, you will bury him in annoyance.

- The insult heaped on a poor man is being heaped on his personal god.
- God is never asleep.
- The day a boy threw away palm oil may not be the day he will be beaten.
- The man who buys meat always for the wife, the day he refuses to buy, the wife will quickly remember the man who would have married her.
- When a woman calls her husband a useless man know that that marriage has collapsed beyond repairs.
- You cannot blame a man in front of the wife.
- Any man who does not know who is stronger than him is yet to grow up.
- As soon as you drop the crab on the ground, it picks race.
- It is improper for a man to swallow a hot nail because he wants to please others.
- It is not proper for a man to burst his scrotum because he wants to sit down.
- It is agonizing for a man that has breast to be sucking stump.
- The sheep that wants to have horns must first of all develop a strong neck.
- The frog that wants to swim in the river should first of all develop strong shoulders.
- The rabbit says instead the predator will apprehend her in her hole, she will prefer taking off from the escape route.

- Whatever that is stolen from the side of a pot usually ends up in the side of the mouth.
- Anyone that blocks the anus should not expect to defecate.
- An elder is not expected to be a spoiler of soup.
- When broomsticks are tied together, they sweep well.
- The man who threw stones at the market square, how sure is he that the parents or siblings are not there.
- The tortoise who went to a native doctor for divination was asked to pay attention while the person the tortoise complained about must also pay attention.
- The food reserved in the broken earthen ware is left for the dog.
- The dog says if he lacks what to do, he starts licking the penis.
- The catechist said he was present when reverend visited and he will be there when he will leave.
- When one person cooks for a community, the community will consume all the supply. However, when a community cooks for one person, he cannot consume it all.
- When meat meant for a clan is not sufficient, the elders will quickly announce that it is a taboo for the women to eat such meat.
- The sun bird says he is an adult, it is only that heart disease has made him appear too small.

- If you did not throw sand at anyone you can hardly be the target of those throwing sand.
- He that brings kola brings life.
- When palm wine embarks on a good mission it will be drank. If on a bad mission it will still be drank.
- If the man that defecated carelessly forgets, the person that packed the faces will not forget.
- You don't climb an Iroko tree twice.
- The fire wood fetched in the dry season is what one uses to warm himself in the rainy season.
- The mother goat that constantly puts to bed twins, how does the pelvic bone look like?
- Everyday is not Christmas.
- You don't climb an Iroko tree with bare hands.
- When a hunted animal makes a swift move, the hunter equally fires at it swiftly.
- instead of the piece of yam on the fire getting spoilt, let the entire fire wood around be exhausted.
- Do not make a mountain out of an anthill.
- If a man defecates on a palm wine tree trunk, the faeces will splash on his body.
- If a man falls inside a pit and raises his hand he may be rescued.
- If you run away from your God, you are still under him.
- If a traveling man defecates on a bush path on his way back, he will be confronted by flies.
- A man who kills with knife does not allow anyone carrying a knife to get behind him.

- He who is entertaining guests is also entertaining himself.
- The nurse of a patient suffers more than the patient.
- The day a man gives up the ghost is not the day he actually died.
- If you don't tell your slave that he is a slave, the day his relations visit, he will tell you he wants to go with them.
- The snake that bit a tortoise has succeeded in biting the shell.
- It is with utmost care that we can kill a tse tse fly that perched on the scrotum.
- A goat, and yam cannot be kept together.
- The visitor invited to eat is now complaining that the host's ball of foofoo is very big.
- The god that showed a little child a yam seedling in a gleaned farm will also give him the tools to harvest it.
- A fowl brought newly into a home stands with one leg.
- Going to Lagos is very easy but leaving Lagos is not easy.
- If the vulture says growing hair on the head is easy let it grow some and let us see.
- The spray meant for the ear is not meant for the eye too.
- With the right hand you smack a child and with the left hand you draw him close to comfort him.
- A hungry man cannot shout Halleluyah.
- The witch cried in the night and the child died in

the morning, there must be a link between the two incidents.

- If you don't own something, you might not likely enjoy it when you want.
- The mushroom that does not want to be uprooted should not spring up.
- It is impossible for a cow to emaciate and have the size of a goat.
- Instead the kola nut will cause strife amongst kinsmen, let them take it to the kolanut tree and share it there.
- When a deity misbehaves, you show him the tree he was carved from.
- When a man vomits, he exposes what he ate.
- When darkness comes it appears as if day light will not come again.
- A wound on the palm does not heal.
- When you expose an illness, it leaves you.
- The old gun has turned into a playing toy for the children.
- When a child speaks an abomination under the cover of the night, he thinks there will never be dawn.
- Whenever you see a dead person lying in state, it is a reminder that one day we shall leave this world.
- It is better to embark on a search for the black goat while there is still day light.
- Locally brewed gin warns that if you assess it with the same eye normally used to assess water it will

show you there is something different between it and water.

- When a man swimming claimed to have dived inside the bed of the river and the back is still seen has he actually dived in?
- It is bad condition that bent the crayfish.
- An advice is only profitable to those who accept it and put it into use.
- Painting someone black behind is more than poisoning.
- It is dangerous for the same person who shouted in the bush to come out and starts asking about who shouted.
- A man who purposely breaks his earthen ware after food, does it mean he will never be hungry again?
- It is good to put a smiling face on a precarious situation.
- A man who cannot afford a bottle of stout beer castigates it as being too bitter.
- A hired sheep keeper will always run away when the lion prods on the sheep.
- There is no way we can leave our buttocks behind while running.
- No person can run faster than his shadow.
- Life is like a market, when you are through with buying or selling you go.
- Anyone that attended Eke Nmegbuoha market (market where the public is maltreated) and returns home to complain about the ill-treatment meted out

to him there, does it mean he did not understand the meaning of the market's name before going?

- It does not pay to wink at somebody in the dark
- The mad man warns that if you want them to start destroying everything around he is ever ready.
- It is better seen how the man with the elephantiasis of the scrotum was slashed with a matchet and how he reacted pronto to the attack. When rice becomes plenty, fowls start selecting it.
- When a big masquerade appears at the market square, everywhere is electrified.
- A praise singer does not sing in vain.
- The man wasting time has an ulterior motive.
- Nobody can be like the atlas that carries the whole world.
- Anyone whose father is in heaven does not go to hell. He who cuts a rock with a knife faces the danger of particles blinding him.
- No one can out grow his culture and tradition.
- Poverty and hardship sharpen one's mettle in life.
- The goat that did not die in infancy will mature to become mother goat.
- \You cannot shave a man's head in his absence.
- The man who killed himself should not expect anyone to weep at his funeral.
- You cannot fully review a book by watching its movie. If not for fools every conversation would have been in proverbs.
- If you tell somebody a proverb and proceed to

explain it to him, the bride price paid on the mother is in vain.

- The kolanut is an illiterate.
- One person alone does not climb the ladder of death
- The fowl that flirts with the hyena does not know that death is in the offing
- An elder who lowers himself like a common commodity will be bought by even children
- The dog has eaten the bone hung on the neck.
- The fowl that ate corn, drank water, swallowed pebbles and sand then turn round to complain of not having teeth, if it developed teeth, will it eat gold?
- The man who visited your home and ate seven pieces of yam and complained of having tooth ache, when the teeth are alright, would he eat a human being ?
- A chick that stands by its mother gets the thigh of the grasshopper.
- A cockroach cannot be safe in the gathering of fowls.
- The man who enjoys eating funeral meat, why does he recuperate from sickness?
- The he -goat said - "Had it been he did not live in his maternal home, he would not have learned to stick the mouth up".
- If you hold the head of a snake, the rest of it is mere rope.
- No matter how long a wooden boat stays in the river, it cannot be a crocodile.
- A child that has the support of the father to steal does not go stealthily, he breaks the door.

- If it were left for only the snail and the tortoise, there would be no gunshot in the bush.
- It is only a foolish man that can carry poison to a purification ceremony.
- You do not stand at one place to watch masquerades.
- If you climb a good tree, you may be given a push.
- A slip of the tongue is more dangerous than a slip of the foot.
- The man who belittles the sickness suffered by a monkey should endeavour to see the swollen eyes his nurse developed through blowing sickness fire.
- When a foolish man is made a bus conductor, he preoccupies himself with waving at everyone on the road.
- The chicken that will mature into a cock can be identified on the first day it hatches.
- No one shows God to a child.
- Marriage is not palm wine to be tasted.
- When a child says while arguing that "my father told me," he has sworn the greatest oath.
- Warring neighbours are quick to become friends in a strange land.
- You do not use the left hand to point the way to your home.
- If the rat cannot run fast enough, it must give way to the tortoise.
- A man without appetite for food should not discourage others with appetite.
- A man who travels regularly should avoid making enemies.

- When a man who climbs a palm tree fouls the air up there, the flies get confused.
- When a masked spirit visits you, you must appease the footprints with presents.
- When an African policeman visits you, you must give him a present, if you visit him, you must go with a present
- If you notice a growing stalk that can pierce your eye, you uproot it and not sharpen it.
- Only a foolish man can preoccupy himself with chasing little bush rodents when his mates are after big games.
- If you have not wrestled with one of those who have made your compound a thorough fare, others will not stop passing through it.
- Whatever drum you beat in a strong man's house you must get someone that will dance to it.
- There cannot be a dream where there is no sleep. When people are complaining about a man bitten by rat, lizard takes money to have his teeth sharpened.
- A man who is ever ready to take insult does not encourage those interested in fighting his cause.
- Whatever dance step that reigns in a man's time, he learns it.
- A wise man does not ignore the message of the gods no matter how foolish it may sound.
- A man who walks ahead of his mates always, may receive bullet.
- An inquisitive monkey receives the bullet first.

- Whatever that ruins a clan and its people begins from their homes.
- A fish starts decaying from the head.
- The millipede that crawls on top of a branch of a felled iroko tree should try climbing the iroko tree and let us see.
- When the head of a house dies, the house becomes an empty shell.
- When cat travels, the mouse becomes king of the house.
- A dying dog does not perceive the odour of excreta any more.
- The lizard is desperate to sit down but the tail does not allow it.
- No matter how much the tortoise tries, it can not cast of its shell.
- No one joins a white garment church with clear eyes.
- Whoever that is fanning trouble is himself a trouble maker.
- For the earthen pot used in cooking for the chameleon is also used for the lizard.
- Man some times is like a funeral ram that must take all the beatings that comes to him without opening his mouth.
- When an old woman stops in between her gyration to point repeatedly at a place, be assured that some time in the past something happened that affected her life.
- Greetings in the harmattan our elders say are usually taken from the fire place.

- Sometimes when we give our child a piece of yam, we ask him to give us a little. Not that we want to eat but we want to test him.
- A man cannot be too busy to break the first kolanut of the day in his stead.
- When a kingdom is mourning its king, it can never be a private affair any longer.
- Those who do not have forgiving spirit should not bother about marriage.
- Marriage is the only institution no body graduates from.
- A mother-in-law should be blind and deaf.
- If you do not like heat, do not enter the kitchen.
- A man's debt to the father in law can not be fully paid.
- If a man sort for a companion that acts like him, he will remain in solitude forever. It is not bravery for a man to beat the wife.
- Never make an early morning appointment with a newly married man.
- A man said he is not bothered that someone else slept with his wife but he is bothered about what was said before they slept together.
- Rain does not fall on one roof alone.
- A man who has never submitted to anything will one day submit to the burial mat.
- It is better to bale the water while it is still ankle deep.
- Even the smallest person can change the course of the future

- It is Impossible to develop eyestrain from looking on the bright sides of things.
- Even if the future does not look rosy to resign oneself to the situation is to be crippled fast.
- The clan where people are quick to inherit a dead man's property, members are not keen in the recovery of a sick member.
- No termite can ever boast of devouring a rock.
- Two rams cannot drink from the same bucket.
- Meat that has fat will prove it when heated in the fire.
- Whoever that sends a child to catch shrew will also give him water to wash his hands.
- No father will send his son to climb a tree for him and take axe to cut the tree.
- No parent will send a child to fetch fire from a neighbour's kitchen and unleash rain on him.

Bibliography and End Note

*Achebe Chinua ; Things Fall Apart - Heinemann
    Educational Books Ltd
    Halley Court, Jordan hill, Oxford
    United Kingdom, 2002

Achebe China ; Arrow Of God, Heineman
    Educational Books (Nigeria) Plc
    Ibadan, 2003

**John J. and Stibbe Mark : The Big Picture,
    Authentic Media, 9 Holdom Avenue
    Bletchley, Milton Keynes
    Buck, United Kingdom, 2003

John J and Stibbe Mark : The Big Picture 2
    Authentic Media, 9 Holdom Avenue
    Bletchley, Milton Keynes
    Buck, United Kingdom, 2003

Rotimi Ola: The gods are not to blame (a play)
    Oxford university press, Ely House
    37 Dover Street, London, United Kingdom; 1975